BRIDGEND LIBRARY AND INFORMATION

3 8030 60141 617 8

Murder at the Miramar

by

Dane McCaslin

Murder at the Miramar

Published by Accent Press Ltd – 2014

ISBN 9781786151339

Copyright © Dane McCaslin 2013

The right of Dane McCaslin to be identified as the author of this work has been asserted by her in accordance with the Copyright, Designs and Patents Act 1988.

The story contained within this book is a work of fiction. Names and characters are the product of the author's imagination and any resemblance to actual persons, living or dead, is entirely coincidental.

All rights reserved. No part of this book may be reproduced, stored in a retrieval system, or transmitted in any form or by any means, electronic, electrostatic, magnetic tape, mechanical, photocopying, recording or otherwise, without the written permission of the publishers: Accent Press Ltd, The Old School, Upper High St, Bedlinog, Mid Glamorgan, CF46 6RY.

BRIDGEND LIB & INFO SERVICE	
3 8030 60141 617 8	
Askews & Holts	4881685
	£19.99
	PYC

The Prologue, or a Brief Explanation of How I Ended Up Where I Did

If you've ever wanted to get out of an awkward circumstance but had no idea how to go about it without incurring an emotional wound or two, welcome to my world. I happen to know how complex it can be, having had not only the bad luck (read 'poor choice') to be involved with a commitment-phobic man but also the threat of a full-blown Burnette Family Reunion hanging over my head like a pall. Being the modern young gal that I am, I opted for a commonsense approach: I turned tail and ran.

I'm getting a bit ahead of the story, though, so let's get the pleasantries out of the way. My name is Augusta Jerusha Burnette. I know, I know: it's a terribly old-fashioned handle for a woman of my age – I'll be twenty-five on my next birthday, for the inquisitive minds out there – and I've always been a bit peeved at my parents for opting to use my christening as a peace offering to my mother's Great-Aunt Augusta Saddler and my father's eldest sister Jerusha. As you might imagine, it really settled nothing because the order of the names became a new source of conflict.

Families. Can't live with 'em, and can't ... well, I think I'll leave it at that.

I am from a minuscule town in the northern part of my state (which shall remain anonymous, to protect the innocent and wicked alike) and, aside from the odd family feud or two, have never had too much in the way of turmoil in my life.

Until David Grant waltzed in, that is, casually snapping up my heart and turning my ingrained moral code on its head. In spite of all the admonitions concerning the wicked wiles of men, I still fell head over heels for a man who not only took my affections but also absconded with my trust: the cad was married, or as he so succinctly put it, 'in a relational flux'. Be that as it may, I still harbored a pathetic bit of hope that he would make his flux permanent in my favor and we would settle down, raise beautiful children, and live happily ever after.

As my best friend, and cousin, Ellie Saddler might say, 'Double ha.'

In due course, it was David's continuous spineless attitude toward commitment that sent me packing. The man rented a nice condo and had planted the idea that I might, indeed, be asked to share it. *Someday,* he had added somewhat vaguely. And then he proceeded to let me know, in a not-so-subtle manner, that 'someday' actually meant 'never' and that, while he'd love to 'remain friends' (cue the nausea), he'd decided that he needed to 'find' himself.

This continuing David-shaped instability, and the upcoming Burnette Family Fiasco, as I tend to think of our reunions, added together to inch me ever closer to the edge of self-imposed madness. So when I came across a classified ad for an 'Assistant to the concierge' at a beachside resort clear at the other end of the state, I applied posthaste and, before I knew it, was wending my way to a summer without commitment-phobic men or family squabbles.

Par for the course, though, I managed to make the proverbial leap from the frying pan and straight into an inferno: the Miramar Resort was keeping a lot of dirty little secrets.

Chapter One

Lest you get the odd idea or two that I was raised in a family where running away from life was the norm, I suppose I should set the record straight, as they say. Ellie and I were first cousins through my mother and her father, who were siblings of the Saddler variety. Since I was an only child and Ellie had two brothers, it was only natural that we should pair up and face the world together.

We'd grown up in a town that is small enough for everyone to know who you are and where you live, which made mischief-making something of a challenge when we were kids. It was a normal childhood, though, filled with school plays and Brownie meetings and church twice on Sunday. We had chores and responsibilities, and never left the house without first making sure the beds were made and the dishes washed.

The Burnettes, my father's side of the family, leaned toward the tree-hugging end of the societal conundrum, so naturally he was concerned with things like saving the spotted owl, growing our own food, and halting world over-population, hence my gig as an only child. I was by no means lonely, though; Ellie was closer than any sister could be, and, like sisters, we alternately fought and made up, a pattern we never broke. When my chance came for flying the coop, Ellie was my biggest cheerleader, one hundred per cent behind my decision to leave, especially when she found out that 'friends and family' could join me at a hugely reduced rate.

The resort itself was, according to the website,

"situated on a long stretch of near-perfect beach and tucked in neatly at the bottom of a sheer cliff", and was luxury incarnate: sunken tubs in every suite; generous king-size beds piled high with six-hundred thread count sheets and fluffy duvets; and freshly baked cookies available around the clock. Who wouldn't want to spend some time there, especially at pennies on the dollar?

I'll admit right off the bat that I was a bit nervous about making the move, even if it did mean getting shot of a problem or two. I'd moved out of my parents' house a couple of years back, following a disastrous stint at the local college (disastrous because I had issues with actually getting to class) and was currently working in the local restaurant/casino. While 'floor hostess' was the official job description, I didn't do a lot of hostessing *per se*. My work days generally consisted of running errands for one of the floor bosses who seemed content to make my life a dash for lattes and dry-cleaning. I didn't complain, though; the pay was good, especially for our neck of the woods, and I could still crash at my parents' house whenever I felt the need for pampering and a meal that consisted of something more than a frozen dinner tossed into the microwave.

Before I knew it, it was time to leave the familial hometown and take wing for more exotic climes. David's farewell was absolutely inane and somewhat pathetic ("I'll try to give you a call, if I get a chance") and Ellie's hug was gleeful.

'You're going to have a blast, AJ. I can just feel it.' Ellie claims to have psychic abilities. I think she's nuts. Most of the time she's way off, but she blithely explains that away by saying that 'the spirits changed their minds'.

Whatever. I love her anyway.

The drive along the coastal highway was beyond gorgeous. We'd just come through one doozy of a winter, and I wanted to get as far from cold weather as possible. I had sunshine for most of the way, and the play of light on water created a horizon that appeared to be made of sparkling diamonds and sapphires. Squat trees hugged the cliff just below the highway, and their touch of green was enough to cut the glare. I found myself smiling widely as I drove, my hair swirling around my face and neck in the breeze that blew in through the open windows. Life, it seemed, was about to two-step its way up the golden staircase.

Eight hours, three large coffees, and two much-needed pit stops later, I arrived in the coastal town of San Blanco, a luxurious slice of real estate that came with a very large price tag and its own series of pristine seafront vacation destinations. My particular target, the Miramar Resort, sat smack dab in the middle of a fancier adaptation of the usual 'Hotel Row'; a sprawling mansion turned 'bed and breakfast' on one side and a well-known golf resort on the other. The elegant façades, combined with a spectacular sunset that tinted the ocean and sky with unbelievable colors, promised a long, lazy summer full of good people, good food, and – best of all – good money.

The valet standing at the front entrance of the Miramar waved me around to a side portico after I had explained who I was and why I was there. I parked and walked in through a double door, still pretty la-di-da for being merely the hired help's access. I glanced around the quiet interior, eyeing the understated elegance that surrounded me. The foyer in which I found myself standing was decorated in a soothing palette of coast-inspired colors, the several paintings on the walls reflecting the muted taste of the designer. There was a faint aroma of the famous cookies that were a part of the resort's signature service, and I suddenly realized that it had been quite a few hours since my last stop for something besides coffee. A freshly-baked oatmeal raisin was sounding pretty good right about then. Or maybe a peanut butter cookie. Or maybe …

A slight noise just behind me turned me on my heel, and I found myself looking into the eyes of an elegantly dressed woman. Her quick glance over my own travel-wrinkled ensemble reminded me that it had been a while since I'd looked in a mirror, and it was all I could do to keep my hands from tugging at clothes and hair. Oh, well. If whoever-she-was didn't like the way I looked, tough luck. I didn't sign up for a fashion show.

'Welcome to the Miramar,' she said in a modulated voice that held just a trace of an accent. 'My name is Esmeralda Ruiz, concierge for the resort. And you are Augusta Burnette, I presume?' She held out s slim hand.

She pronounced my first name with a long vowel sound which, I had to admit, made it seem a bit more exotic than it actually was. I thrust out my own hand in greeting.

'Just AJ, please, Ms Ruiz,' I said with a smile. 'I'm glad to be here. The place is fabulous!' I winced inwardly. I sounded more like a crazed tourist than an employee.

Her face, softened by a sudden smile, lost its look of self-importance and I felt myself relax. 'I agree, AJ. This is a most wonderful place. And I am glad that you're here; I've been up to my eyeballs in work lately.' She rolled said eyes in exasperation, but the smile belied her words. I got the feeling that this woman was a dynamo who would welcome a challenge or two.

'Now, let's get you settled. Do you have luggage?' Esmeralda looked down at the floor as if expecting a suitcase or two to be sitting there.

'I left it in the car,' I answered, motioning toward the doorway. 'If you'll tell me where to park, I can move it and get my bags at the same time.'

Esmeralda Ruiz made a sound that was part snort, part sniff. 'Nonsense. We have staff for things such as that. Let me have your keys and Fernando will take care of it for you.' She held out her hand and I relinquished my keys, cringing inwardly when I thought of the travel clutter that had erupted in my car. I had a sneaking suspicion that Esmeralda's car would be pristine both inside and out.

I waited while she made a quick call from the lobby phone. Speaking rapidly in Spanish, she was apparently not only directing Fernando to move my car and bring in my luggage, but also giving him a tongue-lashing about something else. I turned my head to hide the grin that had snuck onto my face. Esmeralda Ruiz certainly seemed to rule this place with a fist of iron barely covered with the proverbial velvet glove.

Note to self, I thought. Stay on her good side.

With that chore taken care of to her satisfaction, Esmeralda replaced the handset and turned to me with an appraising look. Eyes narrowed to darkened slits, she stood with arms crossed and a slim forefinger tapping her chin. I had no idea what she was looking at and thought I knew exactly how a bug under a microscope would feel. 'Aha!' she exclaimed with a suddenness that made me jump. 'The Palo Verde Suite! That will be perfect for you and close enough to me that I can reach you any time. Follow me, if you will, please.'

And with that pronouncement, she began to stride rapidly down the carpeted corridor, heading deeper into the resort's interior. It was all I could do to keep up. I crossed my fingers that Fernando could find me; I needed a shower in the worst way and he now held all my worldly possessions in his hands. Well, that was a bit of an exaggeration, I admit. But he *did* have all my clean clothes. And my cuddlier-than-a-soft-puppy bathrobe, which I had a sudden hankering for.

Esmeralda made two abrupt turns then paused outside a polished wooden door. A plaque on the wall beside it read, 'Palo Verde', so I put two and two together and got home sweet home. Using a card key pulled from her pocket, Esmeralda opened the door and stepped back to let me enter first.

Somehow I managed to keep my jaws from gaping apart as I looked around my new digs. A stone fireplace dominated the room, flanked by a pair of plush-looking chairs. Along one wall a couch stretched out in absolute luxury, and a corner cabinet held a flat-screened television and DVD player. There was a small alcove containing a table with two chairs, and a door that led to the bedroom, I presumed. All in all, it was gorgeous, a far cry from my first apartment back home. I turned to face my new boss, who had been watching me as I surveyed the suite.

'I almost don't know what to say, Ms Ruiz,' I began. ('Please. Call me Emmy,' she interrupted.) 'This is absolutely lovely. Do all the resort employees have rooms like this?' I gestured around me, my question taking in the suite and its furnishings.

She laughed, a delightful sound that seemed to suit her. 'Oh, no. It is only you and I who live in. The rest of the employees are locals. I must say that I am so glad to have the company of a woman this time.' A trace of tension had crept into her voice; Emmy was thinking of something – or someone – that was not the most pleasant of memories. As quickly as it had appeared, though, the edgy tone was gone, and she was once more the perfect hostess.

'I will leave you to settle in, AJ. Fernando will be here shortly with your luggage. If you want, you can ring for room service. The menu is changed daily but I'm sure that our chef can prepare something for you. Get some rest and I will call for you in the morning.' With a friendly smile, Esmeralda Ruiz backed out of the suite and was gone.

Chapter Two

After a deep sleep fueled by complete exhaustion, followed by a leisurely shower under pulsating streams of steaming water, I was ready to rock and roll. Sometime during the night, a note had been slipped under my front door indicating that breakfast was served in the Palmetto Room, along with a map to the resort and welcome note from the hotel's manager.

I read through the information with an open mouth. In addition to having my meals cooked for me three times a day – and unlimited fresh cookies – I was to have room service. *And* a weekly cleaning by hotel staff. I could not believe my luck: I had landed the job of my dreams. I might not feel too inspired to return to my hometown after all, I thought with a grin. What my parents would say I had no doubt. What Ellie would say was a given as well. What David would say – actually, in the light of how he had treated me, it really didn't matter *what* he might say. (Here I mentally stuck out my tongue at his image – childish but satisfying.)

Emmy didn't appear until I had finished my breakfast and sat relaxing, perusing the local paper. She looked as elegant as she had the night before, but I could see a tiny smudge in the corner of one eye where she had applied her concealer rather too thickly. Well, she did have a huge responsibility as concierge for one of San Blanco's busiest resorts, and I was pretty sure that the last assistant had left some time ago. I mentally straightened my shoulders and lifted my chin: I was ready to help take on some of the tasks that Emmy had been doing alone. I smiled a greeting as she slipped into a chair across from me.

'Good morning, Emmy,' I said. The sunshine, the breeze that wafted in through the room's open French doors, and the delightful breakfast had combined to work their magic on my usual grumpy morning self, and I felt ready to tackle the world. Or at least to take on the Miramar.

Emmy returned my smile, although hers seemed slightly forced. She *was* tired, I thought, and redoubled my efforts to appear cheerful and competent. I had a sneaking suspicion that I was part of the reason she'd had a late night.

'So, what's my first task?' I leaned over my plate to scoop up the blueberry muffin remains on my fingertips. Whoever the baker was, she or he had it all over my sweet mother's attempts. I could actually hear my waistband shrieking in pain as it was strained to its limits. It seemed Emmy had heard it as well but she, apparently, thought it was coming from another direction entirely. She shot to her feet, staring out through the open doors at a small group of people who had circled around another person who was crying and screaming, and in general making quite a fuss.

Great – just what I need on my first day here, I thought grimly as I too arose and followed Emmy's fast pace out of the Palmetto and onto the patio that backed up to the dining room. Trying to keep up with Emmy while attempting to appear unruffled was going to be tougher than I'd imagined.

The woman who was the center of the commotion was weeping hysterically. She was going on about something, but it was difficult to understand her words in between the sobbing and wailing that pierced both my eardrums and my heart. She was either in serious pain or a superb actress. Either way, she was generating interest, the breakfast crowd all agog.

   House security arrived and managed to draw the woman to her feet and guide her to a bench that sat in the shade of an arbor. The bougainvillea that trailed along the ground seemed almost garish in comparison to the woman's pale face, and I felt a sudden uncertainty, rethinking that bit about acting. This was probably not going to be good, judging by her expression.

   Recalling that I was now an employee of the Miramar, I took it upon myself to gently maneuver the gawkers back to the breakfast tables and off of the patio. I closed the French doors, earning a quick look of gratitude from Emmy, and stationed myself just near enough to hear but not to be in the way. I am a human being, after all, full of the usual foibles and, in general, suffering from an overgrown curiosity. At least I had an excuse for eavesdropping.

   There was something about a child. A little girl, from what I could hear, six years old and given to sleepwalking. Her mother, the woman who had been making the ruckus, described her to the security team, telling them that she and her husband had awakened early to get ready for the day and discovered that Leeza, their daughter, was not in her bed, nor was she anywhere in their suite. The front door, locked securely when they had retired, had been standing wide open and there was no sign of the child.

   'My husband,' she began, speaking between hiccups, 'He's out looking for Leeza. She hasn't done that in a while, but usually ...' Her words broke off as another wave of sobs shook her, and I watched as Emmy moved over and sat down beside the distraught mother, slipping an arm around her shoulders and gently murmuring to her.

   'We have the best in security here, Mrs Reilly. Please do not worry. We will find your Leeza, I promise you.' Emmy looked up at the three men, making a swift motion with her head. They turned and left without a word, and I marveled at the control Emmy exhibited even under duress. She was indeed a force to be reckoned with, and I was suddenly confident in her promise to find and return the missing child.

I hesitantly approached Mrs Reilly, stopping just short of the arbor's shade. I wanted to be helpful, to show Emmy that I could be depended upon in a crisis, but for the life of me, I couldn't figure out what to do. I'm known for engaging my mouth before my brain, though, and what I blurted out proved this beyond all doubt. 'Mrs Reilly, could I get you a cookie?'

Emmy craned her neck to look at me, and instead of the rebuke I expected, she merely replied, 'That is a wonderful idea, AJ. Perhaps a couple of our freshest cookies and a cup of tea would be in order. Mrs Reilly,' she said softly to the woman who now quietly sobbed into a wad of tissue, 'Let AJ escort you back to your suite. She will stay with you until we find your little girl.'

Well. That went much better than I had planned. In reality, I didn't *have* a plan until Emmy spoke up. I smiled down at Mrs Reilly and extended a hand to help her to her feet. Without a word, she allowed herself to be guided back to her room. I called room service for a plate of assorted cookies and a pot of hot tea, and I spent the next few moments sitting next to her on the sofa, patting her hand as we waited for the goodies to be delivered.

The only time I could recall a child being lost was when my cousin Edmond, Ellie's older brother, got lost in the local Walmart. It was actually his fault, though; he'd been playing hide and seek with Ellie, hiding among the round clothes racks that stood clustered throughout the store. Aunt Amie had wandered on, intent on her list and baby Brody, only half paying attention to the number of children following in her wake. And, just like that, Ed was lost as a goose.

We still tease him about the fit he threw when he

realized that his mama had left him behind. Ellie, giggling too much to be of any help, couldn't remember the last place she'd seen her brother. When a grumpy store employee, Ed dragging behind her like a recalcitrant puppy, found my near-hysterical aunt, only five minutes had expired. Being lost in the wilds of Walmart was nothing, though, compared to what Mrs Reilly was going through.

A soft tap at the suite's door heralded the arrival of the tea and cookies, and I rose to answer. I was grateful for something to do; sitting still and not talking isn't one of my strong points. The young maid who stood there with the tray didn't bother to hide her curiosity. She gazed past me to stare at the distraught woman on the couch; the news had obviously reached the kitchen. I moved to my left, effectively blocking the view as I took the tray from her.

Mrs Reilly accepted a cup of tea from me and placed it on the table without taking a sip. A warm peanut-butter cookie, though, disappeared quickly. Good sign, I thought, munching my own soft oatmeal raisin. In my opinion, sugar in any form is a sure-fire cure for anxiety, and we certainly could use a dose or two right about then.

Another soft tap sounded and Mrs Reilly instantly stiffened, dropping the remainder of her cookie on the table beside the tea. I stood to my feet, ready to answer the door, but it was flung open before I could get there.

Emmy Ruiz, a sheen of sweat across her forehead, stood holding the hand of a confused-looking little girl, still clad in her princess-patterned nightgown.

Behind her stood a man – Mr Reilly, I presumed – a smile almost splitting his face in two.

Mrs Reilly gave a strangled cry then leapt to her feet, pushing past me and kneeling down on the floor, taking her daughter into her arms. It was a sight fit for a greeting card or a TV commercial, and I slipped past the family reunion and out to the hallway.

A few minutes later, Emmy and I settled ourselves at her desk in the main lobby, the ubiquitous cookies and a pitcher of ice water waiting for us. As joyful as I felt, I noticed Emmy wasn't responding the way I thought she would. I mean, finding a lost child is momentous, and I expected to hear an excited version of how Leeza had been recovered, of the heroic efforts of the security team. Instead, Emmy sat looking at the desk top, not saying a word.

'Emmy?'

She looked up at me, and I could see signs of something – anxiety, or worry, or something more unpleasant – on her face. Things were definitely not right at the Miramar.

'Emmy?' I repeated her name, reaching over to touch her shoulder. 'What's happened?'

She sighed. 'The men, when they found Leeza, they also found ...' Her voice broke off and she dropped her gaze back to her cupped hands as though she'd find the rest of her sentence hiding there. She took a deep breath. 'They found someone else.'

I was a tad confused. Somehow I'd gotten the idea that finding people was a *good* thing, but Emmy was acting like something terrible had happened. My puzzlement must have been evident, and she continued, her eyes looking somberly into mine.

'The person they found, the man – they found him just lying there. Dead.'

It took a moment for that to sink in. A body. A dead body. Not too far from where I sat now, inhaling the scent of freshly baked cookies and basking in the glow of doing a good deed so early in the day.

I gulped hard, trying to think of something comforting to say. The look on Emmy's face, though, said it all: something was really wrong here.

Chapter Three

I honestly had no response to Emmy's statement. The idea that someone had been lying dead not too far from my immediate location gave me the willies, even worse than the time that Ellie slipped a piece of ice down my back during a school assembly. (And then acted all innocent while I was hauled out by the arm, marched to the Principal's office, and read the riot act about interrupting school functions.)

To my credit, I kept my mouth firmly closed. I've never liked that gaping fish look some folks get when ambushed with unpleasant news. Instead, I tried to wrap my mind around the situation, attempting to come up with a nugget of wisdom that would take Emmy's worried look away.

'Do they have any idea who he is? I mean, was he …' I left the unspoken words hanging in mid-air, but Emmy, bless her heart, finished my awkward question with her answer.

'No, he wasn't, at least not that we know of, AJ. We've gone over the guest list and can't find a man staying here alone, and no one has reported a missing husband or boyfriend yet, so we can assume he is not one of ours.' She gave a wry smile, taking a sip from her glass and setting it back on the desk.

I had to think about that one for a minute or two. It made sense, in a roundabout fashion, but then again, just how many murderous spouses or girlfriends would call up the front desk to admit losing someone? Probably no one I knew, except maybe David's wife, but that was another story entirely.

'Unless,' I offered, reaching out for another of those marvelous cookies, 'He was killed off by said girlfriend or wife and she hasn't gotten around to admitting anything yet.'

Emmy looked up sharply at me, an expression I couldn't quite identify on her face. Was it something I'd said? She smiled at me then, and I wondered if I had perhaps misread her.

'Now that would be very interesting, wouldn't it?' She stood to her feet stretching her arms above her head and giving her back a little twist. 'Ah. That's better. Now I need to meet with the detectives and reassure them that this dead man is not ours. Why don't you check out the resort while I take care of that?' She smiled at me then exited the lobby, heading, I presumed, to wherever the detectives were waiting.

I certainly did not need another invitation to stroll through paradise. I picked up two more cookies – pecan chocolate chip and a cinnamon-laced snickerdoodle – before heading out. I never knew when I'd need some more nourishment of the sugary kind.

The sun had moved closer to its noon position in the azure sky, but it still felt fresh. I loved the breeze that came in from the ocean; I even liked the faintly fishy smell. It reminded me of the many trips to the beach we took when I was a child, spending long days scouring the sands for broken bits of shell and, if lucky, a starfish or two. I had kept a collection of those treasures in a mason jar beside my bed, and it retained its seaside smell for a long time after.

At first, I wandered about somewhat aimlessly. The Miramar Resort wasn't a wide piece of property, but it stretched out lengthwise for a ways. The main building sat front and center, of course, and in the daylight I could see several other structures standing on either side. Conference rooms and the like, I presumed, remembering from the brochure that in addition to family-centered vacations, it also provided space for meetings and banquets.

After about fifteen minutes of this, I stopped in the shade of a vine-covered arbor, twin to the one near the dining room's patio. I was getting a bit warm in the sunshine, blaming the heat rather than the unaccustomed exercise, and had just about decided to end my tour when movement near the front of the property caught my eye. From my vantage point, it looked like a monstrous creature, two-headed and many-limbed, and it was heading for the main lobby's entrance.

Not one to be left out of any excitement (in a small town like mine you take it where you can get it), I walked as quickly as I could without being obvious about my target. I really didn't want others to think of me as the resident Nosey Nellie. At least not until I *truly* deserved it.

The lobby seemed to be the epicenter of whatever was happening. I spotted Emmy near her desk, standing straight and speaking calmly with two men wearing what I thought of as 'detective casual': Khaki pants paired with short-sleeved polo shirts. The dead giveaway, however, were the badges swinging from around their necks and the pistols holstered at their sides. Hmm. This was beginning to look like more than a mere body find, and I edged closer, skirting the lobby's perimeter with a stealth that would have amazed Ellie. (In my clan, I have the misfortune to be saddled with the nickname of 'Grace'. I don't possess an ounce of the stuff, hence the sobriquet.)

From where I stood, I could tell that Emmy wasn't as self-possessed as she wanted to appear. The tenseness of her neck and shoulders was a dead giveaway, and the line of concern that had manifested itself between her brows put punctuation to the matter. Esmeralda Ruiz was worried.

I managed to catch her attention, giving her a friendly wave of my fingers, just as the nearer of the two detectives turned around and caught me in mid-waggle. I froze, then dropped the offending appendages to my side. What was it about seeing an officer of the law that set off my guilt alarms? All I had done was wave to a friend, and I felt like I'd just tried to send her a secret message telling her to run for it.

Thankfully, Emmy – once again – saved my bacon. She smiled in my direction, motioning me over to her side.

'Gentlemen, this is AJ Burnette, my assistant. I'm sure she'd love to answer any questions you might have for her, although I must warn you she only arrived last night.' Emmy leaned over and gave my shoulders a light squeeze, then continued. 'I cannot imagine what she must think of us. We do not usually have such goings-on at the Miramar.'

'I would hope not,' said Detective Baird dryly (I could read his name on the official-looking ID that was clipped to his polo's collar.) 'If you don't mind, Miss Burnette, I've got just a few quick questions and then we'll be out of your hair.'

He smiled down at me and I stared in fascination at the lone dimple that popped up out of nowhere. Well, technically it was in his left cheek, but his stern demeanor had managed to keep that little quirk under wraps.

I dragged my eyes upward, and I could see amusement in his baby blues. I felt myself blushing, and I knew it wouldn't be a dainty hint of color in my cheeks, either. I tend to do things a bit over the top, and my blushes are no exception.

Now that I thought about it, even David had never managed to elicit such a blush. In fact, I couldn't recall a single time when he made me feel anything more than just a mite past ordinary. Even his eyes were nothing to write home about. David's eyes were hazel. No, wait – they were brown. I almost lost track of what I was doing at that moment, so amazed was I at the trouble I had even recalling something as simple as his eye color. Maybe I *was* beginning to get over the cad. Ellie would be so pleased.

'AJ?' Emmy's face swam in to focus in front of me, and I saw that she had that concerned look again. She was probably wondering what kind of a nutcase she'd hired.

'Yes. I mean, no.' I said, sounding as confused as I felt. 'No, I do mean yes.'

Fabulous. I was sounding a mite *loca,* as the locals would say. I could see Detective Baird had guessed the reason behind my discomfort or, at least, I thought he had. Why else would he flip on the dimple switch again?

Emmy's hand tightened a bit on my shoulders. I could tell she thought that she had a loony tune on her hands. I needed to dispel that idea but quickly.

I managed to let out a laugh. Mind you, it sounded more like a cat with its tail caught in a screen door than the delicate tinkle I might have preferred, but it served its purpose. Emmy's hand relaxed and Detective Baird tucked the devastating dimple away for another time. It was all business now.

'Do you mind ...?' I indicated a trio of chairs clustered together for a cozy chat near a window. 'I need to sit down for a moment.' Let them think I was a silly female with "the vapors", as my Grandma Tillie might say. I really *was* tired from the unfamiliar exercise I'd just had. Walking in sand can be tough work on underused calf muscles.

Baird nodded and I led the way, taking the chair that faced away from the window and towards Emmy's desk. Apparently, Baird had the same idea (you know what they say about great minds and all that jazz) and moved his chair next to mine, both of us looking at Emmy now. I supposed that was to keep us from exchanging secret signals or something sinister like that. After all, he *had* caught me waggling my fingers at her.

'Let's begin with the time you arrived last night.' This was from the other detective, the one who had left his chair quite alone and was sitting with his back to Emmy but facing me head-on.

I squinted to read his badge (I hate to admit that my eyes are less than perfect, not wanting to mar my visage with clunky frames). Without changing his expression – and thankfully not having a dimple to flash – he flipped his ID around and held it so I could see it. Through slightly scrunched eyes I managed to see the words 'Detective Fischer' and I blushed again, but this time squelched it in mid-spread. All I needed was another dimple episode, courtesy of Detective Baird.

I wrinkled my forehead in a show of concentration. I am a great believer in expressive body language, so I figured if I looked like I was thinking, they'd make this quick.

'It was just after seven – no, it was already eight. That's right. I noticed the time when I pulled into the Miramar. I wanted to call Ellie and tell her how long it took me to get here.' I was babbling. I also believe wholeheartedly in the theory that if you give someone enough rope, or in my case, words, they'll hang themselves. I was doing a beautiful job of tying knots at the moment.

Detective Baird had stopped making marks in his little notebook. I was either holding the man in complete thrall, or else he was assessing my mental health. I had a sneaking suspicion which one it was, which threatened to begin the whole blushing thing all over again.

'Was it seven or eight? We need you to be as specific as you can be, OK?' He gave an almost imperceptible shake of his head. I managed a quick peek out of the corner of my eye and noticed the way his hair had curled behind his ears and over his collar.

Get a grip, AJ, I sternly admonished myself. This

interview would turn disastrous but quick if I kept letting my mind wander over Detective Baird the way I had strolled around the Miramar.

'Eight. Definitely eight. I left home at noon and it took eight hours to get here, just like Ellie said it would, so that's why ...' I left the sentence unfinished, feeling, rather than seeing, Baird's shoulders tense as I stepped off the conversational path once more.

'OK. Eight it is.' This came from Detective Fischer. I turned to face him, glad for a reason to focus on someone else for a change. If this little *tête-à-tête* lasted much longer, I'd be checking out Baird's ring finger as well.

Chapter Four

To my credit – or probably more to my mother's, since it was she who had drilled me in public etiquette since I was a mere tyke – I managed to stay seated until the two detectives left the lobby. As soon as they passed through the entrance, though, I bounced to my feet and beat a hasty path to Emmy's desk.

She was still sitting where I'd left her, and the file she had pulled from the cabinet behind her desk remained unopened, her hands folded on top of it. I hesitated, not knowing whether or not this was the right time to interrupt her reverie. I have never been accused of having perfect timing, though.

'Hey, Emmy?' I plopped down into the chair next to her desk. 'You OK?'

She looked at me as if she had just noticed my presence, her troubled eyes on mine. 'Yes, thank you, AJ. I'm just thinking. So,' she made an effort to perk up, 'What did the detectives ask you about?'

'Besides name, rank, and serial number?' I joked.

She seemed genuinely interested, so I proceeded to give her a slanted version that probably wouldn't match Detective Dimple's notes. I wanted to see her smile.

'Oh, just the usual questions about who dun it and what time I got here last night. I think they were trying to pin it on the new girl.' I paused and looked down at the empty plate that should have been filled with fresh cookies. 'Hey, what's up with the hired help? Did they forget us or what?'

Emmy smiled then, looking more like her normally in-control self.

'I've noticed your sweet tooth, AJ. Would you like me to ring for more?' Her hand moved toward the unobtrusive slim phone that sat near her computer.

'No, that's OK,' I laughed. 'I know where they're hiding.' I stood to my feet, feeling a little better about Emmy's frame of mind. 'I need to run to my suite anyway but I'll be back shortly. Can I stop by and pick something up for you, maybe a sandwich or something?'

Emmy shook her head. 'I'm fine, AJ, but thank you. I have a few calls to make, so take your time.' With that, she picked up the phone and began to dial, smiling a dismissal.

I left the main lobby and took the quickest route to the back corridors leading to the various suites and guest rooms. I needed to unpack my bags and get my laptop hooked up; thank heavens for free Wi-Fi, I thought, with a smile. I could Skype with Ellie later on, assuming I'd have time to myself that evening.

Still marveling at my complete luck in finding such a job, I quickly settled my things and, after a nanosecond of hesitation, rang for some lunch. I mean, if it came with the territory, then why not? I banished the guilt and settled down to wait for my turkey, Swiss, and avocado croissant, feet propped up on the coffee table and head pressed back into the deliciously soft couch cushions. This was something I could get seriously used to in a hurry.

I must have dozed off without even realizing it because the knock at my door pulled me to my feet with a jerk. The same little maid from this morning stood there, her face filled with a curiosity to make the Saddler nosiness look downright proper. What was she expecting to see? More bodies? Maybe a corpse or two in my suitcases or tucked behind the couch?

That thought brought me up short. Maybe she looked that way at me because they were already talking in the kitchen. An uncomfortable feeling slithered over me like an unwelcome snake and I all but snatched the plate from her hand, shutting the door with the briefest of thank-yous. If that were the case, I'd have to set someone straight and do it quickly before they had me turned into the assistant of Frankenstein. Why do folks always blame the new kid on the block?

After getting the food down – which was delicious, by the way – I felt somewhat better. Breakfast had been a long time ago, according to my internal clock, not counting the cookies I'd downed as a preventative against shock. I was still trying to decide what to do next when my suite's phone rang, startling me into the present.

'Hello?' I said into the handset. Who, besides Emmy, would be calling me? With no response, I tried again, assuming that whoever had dialed my number might not have heard me answer. 'Hello, this is AJ.'

The unmistakable sound of dial tone buzzed in my ear and I replaced the handset on the phone's base. Weird, but nothing to become unhinged over, I decided. Folks often rang wrong numbers, then disconnected without explanation.

I was just stepping through the front door when the phone rang again, halting me in mid-stride. This time it *was* Emmy, and she needed me to help her get a group of conventioneers set to rights. I promised her I'd be right there and left my suite, careful to lock the door behind me. One could never be too cautious, even at a ritzy place like the Miramar.

I joined Emmy at her desk, helping to sort out the milling throng of middle-aged women who stood chatting and laughing as they waited for packets containing information about the resort and the surrounding area. When Emmy had mentioned 'conventioneers', I had pictured a gaggle of old men, *sans* hair save the little strands glued onto the scalp, in business attire, carrying leather briefcases and the Wall Street Journal. This group was in town for the Scrapbooking Extravaganza and instead of briefcases, each clutched large quilted bags of scrapbook goodies as tightly as if they held gold.

With the women sent on their merry way, each now enjoying a cookie or two, Emmy and I sat down. Concierge work, I was rapidly discovering, was not only varied, it could be downright tiring. I looked over at Emmy, carefully noting the dark areas under her eyes. She looked exhausted, and I knew that our day was only half over. Maybe she was ill.

As if sensing my questioning glance, Emmy looked at me and smiled. The lines that radiated from around her eyes seemed new, and I was struck at the difference a day could make in a person's face. It had certainly done so on Emmy's.

'So. That is done. We have one more large party arriving at six then we can have our dinner. Did you have something for lunch?' She arched a brow at me, one hand hovering over the empty cookie plate.

I had to smile. 'Yes, I did. The food here is so good, Emmy. How in the world do you stay so thin?' I nodded at her slim arms that rested on the desk top and she smiled.

'Oh, I think that I run it off, taking care of all these folks,' she said with an expansive wave. 'You will see, AJ. Some days we're on our feet from sun up to sun down and can barely grab a bite to eat.'

She had a point. Aside from the few minutes I'd spent wandering the Miramar and the half hour or so in my suite, I had stayed busy all morning. I glanced at my watch and was surprised to see the little hand pointing at the two. Good lord, Emmy wasn't kidding. This job was a bit more than smiling at guests and handing out cookies. The twinge of guilt I'd experienced at calling Room Service fled for good. I deserved it.

Emmy and I spent an hour or so replacing the stock of

brochures and folders, having handed out most of them to the scrapbooking bunch. There were a few guests who drifted over to the desk to ask for directions to different attractions, or to ask questions about the beaches and whether or not there were lifeguards on duty, but for the most part we worked on in a comfortable silence. At last, Emmy sighed and sat back in her chair, placing her hands to the small of her back and stretching.

'There. I think we are done, AJ. We only need to check on the evening entertainment. I want to see if the sound system has been set up as I requested.' She stood to her feet, groaning softly as she lifted her arms above her head. 'Ah. What I wouldn't give for a good massage just now.'

I looked up at her, an idea percolating in my ever-enterprising brain. 'Is there something I could do? I mean, so you could at least lie down a bit? I would be happy to, really.' I sounded like an acolyte eager to please the master, but I really did want to earn my keep.

Emmy smiled. 'No, but thank you, AJ. You have already been more of a help than you know.'

I nodded, only slightly disappointed. As I've mentioned before, I often engage my mouth without the benefit of brainpower. I stood to join her but she waved me off.

'No, there's nothing you can do right now. Since this is your first day and I don't want you to quit on me just yet, why don't you go and make use of our spa? We have a private area for women only and you'll probably be in there by yourself right now. We can meet up at five,' she added, consulting her watch. She must have read my hesitation, because she added, 'Really, AJ. We'll have a busy evening, so take advantage of this time, OK?'

I smiled my thanks at her and watched her leave the lobby and step out into the afternoon sunshine. She didn't have that usual briskness, I saw, and I felt anxiety for this woman who I'd met only last night. Esmeralda Ruiz struck me as someone who was truly concerned about those in her care, and that she tended to carry a bigger personal responsibility than she would admit. After a morning such as we'd had, I could hardly say I blamed her. Hopefully, she'd have a good night's rest and a much better day tomorrow.

Chapter Five

The evening's entertainment was in full swing, the salsa music swimming upward to sway the bright stars that had begun to appear in the sky. Happy couples danced on the patio and makeshift dance floor, and the musicians kept them asking for more. I sat to the side of the bandstand, watching the guests enjoy themselves. I could feel the day's tension begin to slip away with the music, although I'm certain the glass of excellent Merlot I held was helping as well.

Emmy sat next to me, head tilted back and eyes closed as she listened to the music and the happy chatter surrounding us. I had noticed a lift in the tenseness of her shoulders after she'd returned from checking on the sound system and making sure that all was in place for this evening. She deserved to have things go right for once on this crazy day.

A loud popping noise, accompanied by a brilliant blue flash, startled me from my reverie. Screams from the dancers replaced the pulsating music, and I could see activity was centered near the keyboardist. He now sat slumped forward, his forehead resting on the keyboard and his hands hanging limply down at his sides.

Emmy pushed past me, signaling to the servers to keep the guests back from the bandstand and to clear the dance floor. I was beginning to think this place was jinxed: a lost child; a dead body; and now this latest disaster.

I watched as Emmy, moving with purpose but very carefully, approached the other musicians who seemed frozen where they stood, each staring at their keyboard player as if he'd suddenly sprouted another head. I hurried to Emmy's side, getting there just as one of the security guards arrived. He put a hand on Emmy's arm, keeping her from moving any closer.

'Ms Ruiz, don't mess with that. There could still be live wires on stage. We've called 911 already, so let's just keep the rest of the band away from Miguel, OK?'

He began motioning the musicians to step off the bandstand, and they did so with some reluctance, glancing back to where their bandmate still sat.

Oh boy, I thought. Things were not looking too good for poor Miguel. He hadn't moved at all, aside from a few twitches of his arms and legs. Definitely *not* a good sign.

The faint wail of an approaching siren announced that help was near, and I felt a little better. Once they were here and had things under control, we could continue the party, right? I looked at Emmy to gauge her mindset, and was shocked to catch a look of satisfaction on her face. As quickly as it was there, though, the look was gone, and I was sure I'd been mistaken. It was probably just a trick of the light. Emmy would never be happy to see someone hurt, least of all someone she had hired to represent her beloved Miramar.

The paramedics arrived and assessed it was safe to move Miguel and lay him down on the ground behind the stage. By this time, we'd managed to get the guests rounded up and moved to another venue; a smaller patio around the corner, where a hasty drinks table had been set up. Smart move, I thought approvingly, smiling at the servers who were busy handing out glasses of wine; a little bit of lubrication and hopefully no one would find any of this odd. To be on the safe side, though, I crossed my fingers. And toes. I was just reaching for my own glass when I heard my name.

'Ms Burnette? Do you have a minute?' The familiar

voice from somewhere behind me sent a chill down my spine and not just because I was startled. It was that Detective Dimple again, and I was in his crosshairs.

Slowly, I turned to find him standing just a few feet away, arms folded across his chest and feet planted apart. I didn't see one hint of that intriguing facial feature, though; in fact, he looked rather stern at the moment. That probably wasn't a good omen.

'Well, hey there, Detective. Two visits in one day from the boys in blue have got to be some kind of record for the Miramar.' I was aiming for flippant and managed to sound petulant, as if having the law on the property was some kind of albatross.

He didn't get the joke, either. Instead, motioning me to follow him, he turned and headed for the main lobby's entrance, striding too fast for me to keep up. I guess he thought I had more information, although about what I had no idea. Certainly not Miguel's misfortune; that had been a simple accident, a crossing of some wires. I sighed, looking down at my watch. Eight o'clock. A mere twenty-four hours since my arrival and already having my second police interview. Not an auspicious beginning, I'd say.

When I did manage to catch up, Detective Baird was standing near Emmy's desk, caught with his hand in the cookie jar. Actually, it was the cookie plate, which had been refilled while we were all outside enjoying the music and the evening. He grinned when he saw me, a trace of chocolate on his mouth. I had a sudden desire to kiss it off, then blushed at my own crazy thoughts. What in the world was wrong with me? Unless I was having some post-David reaction, it was just plain wrong to think that way about a police officer. There was probably some law against it anyway.

'How can I help you, Detective?' I didn't mean to sound as cool as I did, but I was over-compensating for my unruly mind. And I was unexpectedly tired. This entire day was taking its toll on me.

Seating myself beside Emmy's desk, I reached for my own cookie, snagging a luscious double chocolate chip. There was enough sugar there to sweeten my mood for at least a week, but if it was working, I couldn't tell. I looked at him as I munched away, waiting for his response. I was determined to keep my mouth shut until I absolutely had to speak.

He leaned on the corner of the desk, licking the remainder of the cookie from his fingers, staring at me thoughtfully. Well, two could play the silent game, mister, I thought to myself, reaching for another cookie. I figured if I kept eating, I couldn't talk.

Finally he relented, heaving a deep sigh to show me how put-upon he felt. 'Look, Ms Burnette, I need to know who was near the sound equipment today. Let's start with you.' He paused, drilling me with those baby blues and I completely forgot what I had been doing that afternoon. Fortunately, his partner walked in just then, giving me a moment to regroup. I was determined to not to appear imbecilic again.

'Hey, Baird. Got a minute? I have something you might find interesting.' Detective Fischer gave me a cursory glance, effectively dismissing my presence. I didn't care; hopefully I would get the scoop on what had happened to poor Miguel.

To my immense disappointment, Baird and Fischer walked off a ways, Fischer murmuring his information in a low voice. In spite of my acclaimed hearing prowess, I couldn't make out a single word. I contented myself with another cookie and surreptitious glances at Detective Baird's backside. Definitely worth the wait, I reflected.

In spite of his ability to hold my attention in thrall, I was able to come up with a timeline of my day. I had a feeling that I would not be able to wriggle out of this little conversation despite the cookies.

Heels clicking on the marble floor made me look around. Emmy stood at the entrance and I could see instantly that something was wrong. She looked upset to the point of weeping, and I sprang to my feet, wanting to go and comfort her. Detective Fischer had other ideas, though, and stepped neatly into my path as I tried to scoot past.

'We still need to talk with you, Ms Burnette, so it's probably not a good idea.' What did the man think I would do? Grab Emmy's hand and run off into the darkness? Come up with matching stories so we could alibi each other? I really thought he was smarter than that. I gave him the most disparaging look I could muster and turned back to my chair, walking with shoulders soldier-straight and chin thrust out to indicate my contempt. This was becoming unbearable.

I was eventually allowed to go to my suite – I say 'allowed' because, at one point, Detective Baird left in a hurry and the irritating Detective Fischer remained behind as a babysitter for me and for Emmy, who had taken a seat on the other end of the lobby. Even from where I was, I could see the dejection in the slump of her shoulders and I wondered what had happened (besides all the pandemonium we'd had already) to make her feel that badly.

The message light on my room's phone was blinking madly, bathing my room with an eerie blood-colored effect. I shook my head. I really needed to lighten up. Today had been bad – awful, really – but surely we'd reached our quota of murder and mayhem, enough to last a year or two.

'AJ! Call me! I need to talk to you pronto!' That was Ellie, sounding urgent. I smiled. Ellie got riled up over what to eat for dinner. I hit 'Delete' and moved to the next message.

'AJ! I mean it! Call me!' Ellie again. Hmm. I deleted

that one as well, but was beginning to get that prickly feeling on the back of my neck. Ellie usually settled down after the first call; two in a row seemed a bit much, even for her.

When the third message began to play, the prickle morphed into a chill. It was Ellie again.

'AJ! Please! I have a really awful feeling! Please call!' Whatever she was worked up about, it was making its way through the phone lines and right up my spine.

I managed to find my cellphone, only to discover I'd forgotten to charge it overnight. I threw it down on the couch beside me, irritated I'd let the battery die. A burst of inspiration hit me – Skype! Actually, I told myself, that would be better than just a phone call anyway; I'd be able to see Ellie's expression and figure out if she was having one of her anxiety attacks or was really on to something.

My laptop was already plugged in, thank goodness, so I booted it up and tapped my fingers impatiently on the keyboard as I waited for the screen to come to life.

I was in luck. The flashing icon at the bottom of the Skype window announced that Ellie was already online. I sent her an instant message, clicking on the 'Open Conversation' button as I did. She popped onto my screen, slightly off-center and fuzzy.

'Hey, cuz! What's with all the phone messages?' I tried to keep my voice light. When Ellie was in one of her 'moods', as we called them, there was no talking her down off whatever emotional ledge she'd climbed out onto.

'AJ, you need to come home and I mean now.' Ellie's faced looked pinched with worry, and my insides turned to jelly. Was it my parents? Or David? (Although I wasn't certain that I cared just then.) I felt my stomach tighten as I waited for her to clarify.

'What's happened, Ellie? Is everything OK at home?' I know I probably looked as freaked out as I felt.

Ellie gave a small laugh. 'Everything's fine here, AJ.

It's that place you're at that has me worried. I did a reading this evening and I see nothing but trouble for you if you stay there.'

Let me explain that Ellie, in addition to being convinced she has psychic abilities, also thinks she can 'read' the future in that crazy pack of oversized cards she carries everywhere. I've seen her at work, laying out the cards in a particular pattern, flipping them over one by one and telling me what they meant. I had to chuckle. If that was all, I could relax.

'I'm serious, AJ.' The downside of Skyping was that the person you were talking with could see you as well as you could see them, and she'd seen the amusement on my face. 'You need to get back here ASAP. I've got a real bad feeling about that place.'

I hesitated. Should I tell her what had already happened in just the first twenty-four hours? Probably not the best of ideas, I concluded. I smiled at her image on my screen.

'Ellie, if anything happens here, I'll hightail it home as fast as I can go, OK? Promise.' I tried to throw as much reassurance behind my voice as I could, because Ellie was like a dog with a bone if she thought someone was ignoring her good advice.

She made a snorting sound of disgust. 'AJ, you *always* promise to stay out of trouble. I'm beginning to think you have a built-in magnet for the stuff.'

She had a point. When we were growing up, if there was mischief to be made or found, I was usually in pole position.

'Look, Ellie,' I said firmly. 'Nothing's happened to me. I have to admit there've been a few bumps …' I broke off as Ellie jumped on my words like vultures drawn to a kill.

'I knew it!' she said triumphantly. 'The cards never lie.' She leaned back in her desk chair and crossed her arms, a look of self-congratulation on her face. When Ellie felt vindicated, the whole world could tell.

That did it. Here I was, a woman grown and out on my own (finally), and my goofy, card-reading, spirit-seeing cousin wanted to sabotage me. She was just jealous that she wasn't down here, living it up in a private suite with room service and attractive detectives to boot. I put my foot down, both literally and figuratively.

'Eleanor Louise Saddler! I have about had it up to here with your crazy predictions!' I had built up a fine head of steam and was determined to vent every last bit of it at the smug face on the computer.

Thankfully, Ellie neither batted an eye nor returned my ire. I really didn't want an argument with her. Instead, she merely shrugged and turned off her end of the connection. Well. If that didn't beat all. It just goes to prove you can never predict what someone is going to do.

Chapter Six

There was no two ways about it: the conversation with Ellie had rattled my cage more than I cared to admit. Not that I believed she could predict the future or anything like that, but it was weird she was getting bad vibes from the Miramar. I knew the problems here were definitely not your average, run-of-the-mill type, but I was beginning to get an undercurrent of something that set me on edge. Maybe she had something there.

Or maybe she was just jealous. That was always a possibility, knowing Ellie as I do.

Right now, though, I wanted to make sure that Emmy was all right. I was really worried about her, especially considering the way she had slumped in that chair, all the starch gone from her posture. Troubles did that to a person, I knew; and I also knew that, if she let them, they'd beat her down to the ground.

I turned off my laptop and placed it back on the coffee table, glancing at my watch: seven-fifty five. Emmy would probably still be in the main lobby, even if the two detectives had already gone. I had a hunch that she was one of those types who worked themselves silly whenever their world was atilt.

I hurried out of my suite and headed back through the corridors, my footsteps muffled by the thick carpet. This was one of the nicest joints I'd even been in, and even the floors got the five-star treatment. Too bad things were so out of kilter, though.

I was right. Emmy was at her desk, a thick stack of

folders in front of her and the computer screen glowing brightly. I could tell she was concentrating on something so I tried not to startle her as I approached. Another jolt to her system might not be too wise.

'Ah, AJ,' Emmy said as I edged up to her desk. She rubbed her eyes, stifling a yawn with manicured fingertips. 'I am so sorry. Today has been hectic, to say the least. What can I do for you?' She smiled up at me, and I could see that the shadowy smudges underneath her eyes were darker than they had been earlier.

'I thought I'd get us a glass of wine, maybe something to munch on, if that's kosher with you.' I waited for the go-ahead, hoping she'd agree. Too much work was never good, in my opinion.

Emmy suddenly smiled, a brilliant rainbow peeping out through a haze of gloom. 'That's a wonderful idea, AJ. In fact, let me order it. Do you prefer red or white?' She reached for the phone on her desk, one eyebrow lifted in question.

'Red, please. No, white. And some sugar cookies as well, if there are any.' I grinned. I could handle anything with a glass of wine and a cookie.

Emmy shook her head, smiling, the lines of tension between her brows smoothing out. 'You need your own personal baker, AJ.'

As I've said, I have long felt that sugar – especially in the guise of soft, chewy, warm-from-the-oven cookies – can be a mood-changer. And I happened to be having a five-cookie anxiety attack at the moment, never mind my infamous sweet tooth.

While she ordered up our treats, I wandered over to the wide windows that overlooked the sweeping drive. I couldn't see the dance floor from where I was standing, but the glow of portable floodlights could be seen, reflecting off the buildings and shrubbery. I shuddered. What were the odds of finding two dead bodies in one day? Granted, one was an accidental discovery and the other an outright misfortune, but still.

It was nerve-wracking, to say the least. I remembered my determination to cheer Emmy up and forced my features into a neutral expression. It wouldn't help to have her reading my thoughts just then.

'It will be here in just a minute, AJ. Shall we stay in here or go outside?'

I was surprised. I didn't think she'd want to be out where the investigation was still ongoing, and I didn't relish the risk of getting on Detective Fischer's hit list again. (Now Detective Baird – that was a horse of a different color altogether. I'd get on *his* list any day.) I opted for outside, Detective Fischer be hanged. I had wine, cookies, and a mission.

We managed to fly beneath the radar, strolling along the outside of the grounds and down toward the beach. A few hardy souls were still out there, braving the chill, splashing and running through the waves, but for the most part we were alone. Emmy was quiet, pensively sipping her wine as we walked. The moon, just coming up over the cliffs, shone golden in the sky, and a light breeze had kicked up, making me glad I'd thrown on a sweatshirt.

'What do you think happened back there tonight?' I motioned with my chin toward the resort and the floodlights.

'I wish I knew.' Emmy's voice was quiet. 'He was a friend, AJ. I knew Miguel for a long time. I'd even gotten the job for him when he worked here.'

That was news to me. I had no idea he'd worked at the Miramar before. Maybe I'd misunderstood.

'You mean the gig tonight?' I glanced at Emmy as I sipped my Pinot Grigio, waiting for her answer.

She shook her head. 'Miguel worked here for a few months in the springtime, but ... well, things happened and he left. I didn't blame him, though,' she added hastily.

'Miguel was a good man, a family man. His wife will be so sad.' She shook her head.

'Life can be truly crappy, Emmy. I hope whoever lets her know is nice about it.' I could picture Detective Fischer's dry delivery of the facts, not knowing what to do with a weeping woman. Detective Baird would know exactly what to say and do, of that I was sure. How could a man with a dimple ever be unkind?

'What kind of job did Miguel do when he was at the Miramar?' My inability to let something go had kicked in, and I was curious why anyone would leave the resort.

Emmy slowly took another mouthful of her Chardonnay, eyes fixed on the horizon. 'He was my assistant.'

I took that in for a moment, letting the words chase one another around my addled brain. He was me? Or rather, I was now him? What in the world might have sent Miguel off to find employment elsewhere after working at the Miramar? I wasn't complaining, mind; I was glad to have this job. I just couldn't imagine a dust-up with Emmy, though, especially not after seeing them talking together earlier.

A filigree mist was slowly curling in from the water and the breeze had quickly developed into a sturdier version of its former self. I shivered, pulling the sweatshirt's hood over my head. I could never handle cold ears, and mine were definitely in the icy range.

Emmy shivered slightly, drawing a thin cardigan more firmly around her body. 'Maybe we should turn back now, AJ. It's getting colder and I still have so much to finish this evening.'

We strolled back toward the Miramar, past the floodlit patio with its reminder of the evening's tragic events. I shivered, too, but not from the cold. Miguel's death made me think I hadn't heard everything there was to hear about his past employment and relationship with Emmy.

And Detective Baird made me shiver for altogether another reason.

I have a healthy belief that passing the buck can be both good and bad, and I have had extensive practice in both. However, my first day at the Miramar was beginning to feel like one huge experiment in the blame game. Emmy blamed herself for Miguel's demise, Detective No-Personality Fischer had hinted at everyone being a suspect, and I was beginning to think I'd blundered into a B-rated crime movie, which, of course, was Ellie's fault. If she hadn't encouraged me ... well, between that and David's irritating behavior. I sincerely hoped his wife would take him back and let me off the hook.

After I'd returned to my room following our impromptu beach stroll, I considered Skyping Ellie again and decided against it. I was tired, I was a bit tipsy, and I was ready to sleep. Hopefully tomorrow would be a regular day at the Miramar, since my first day certainly wasn't. I hoped.

Chapter Seven

I could sense light in my eyes. Something had awakened me and I lay there for a moment, slightly dazed and trying to decide if it was already morning. I thought I could hear movement, a shuffling noise, and oddly enough, the light seemed to be moving, flickering off and on.

Here goes nothing, I thought, and sat up in bed, switching on the bedside lamp in one swift movement. A loud clinking sound, like metal against glass, could be heard: someone was definitely in my suite. I slid from the covers as stealthily as I could, managing to catch one foot in the trailing sheet and tripping myself. Great.

The noises ceased. I froze, trying hard not to breathe, straining my ears to listen for something to give me a clue as to who had decided to make themselves at home in my private quarters. They must have been listening for me as well. Drawing in a deep breath, I jumped through the open bedroom door, leaping like a deranged frog at the figure that was leaning into my refrigerator.

I'm pretty sure that I squealed the louder. Ellie was a close second, the two of us jumping sky high as we ran smack-dab into each other.

'Oh, my God! Ellie! What in the world are you doing here?' I exclaimed, trying to regain my balance and clutch my chest at the same time. 'And how in the world did you get in?' So much for tight security, I grumbled to myself.

Ellie can recover quickly from surprise. She demonstrated this talent for me by leaning casually on the kitchen counter, crossing her arms and giving me her famous glare.

'I would think you'd be happy to see me, AJ,' she said huffily, eyes narrowing and brows drawn together. Ellie is also one of the world's worst for getting offended over nothing.

'I am, Ellie, I'm just – well, how in the world did you even know where my room was?' Ellie had a knack for getting into places – she'd done this sort of thing before. It still didn't explain how she found me so easily, though.

That came out sounding like I was hiding out, trying to avoid her, not the smartest move when trying to defuse her bad temper. Simple conversations could become a test of walking on eggshells whenever Ellie was in one of her moods. I was digging a deep verbal hole and doing it fast. I looked around the room for a distraction, still feeling a bit discombobulated, what with being awakened by Ellie sneaking in like a burglar and then almost having a heart attack in my own kitchen. And the only answer I'd got from her was an exaggerated eye roll: Ellie could be incredibly tight-lipped when she wanted to be.

'What time is it?' I asked, brushing unruly hair from my face and wrapping my arms tightly around my middle. It was awfully chilly in my suite.

'It's a little past four,' Ellie answered, apparently deciding to forgo the huffiness for a moment.

'Four? As in "four in the morning"?' I exclaimed, looking at her incredulously. 'What in heaven's name made you drive all the way down here in the middle of the night, Ellie?'

'Well, that's gratitude for you,' Ellie said, addressing the ceiling. 'I came down here, AJ, because I know you're in danger.'

I snorted. 'I am not in danger, Ellie. The Miramar is perfectly safe. And you *did* come down here on your own accord,' I pointed out ungraciously. 'So you can't be *that* afraid to be here.'

Ellie harrumphed, turning back to the fridge and opening it once more. Along with possessing mercurial moods, Ellie has a metabolism that allows her to eat more than any single being I know and not have any lasting damage to show for it. I, on the other hand, only have to *think* about chocolate and I gain weight. (Note to self: slow down on the cookies.)

I yawned. Clearly Ellie was here to stay and I was past going back to bed. I could use something to wake me up since, apparently, my day had already started.

'I can call for something to eat, maybe get us some coffee, Ellie,' I offered.

There is nothing like food for a peace offering, especially with Ellie. Over the years I've gotten to be quite the master of judging what kind of goodies will bring her out of a sour mood and back on friendlier terms.

'You have room service? *And* this suite?' She practically screeched the words at me, gesturing dramatically around the room, taking in the fireplace and flat screen television.

I smiled smugly. 'Yep. And housekeeping service once a week, too.' Ellie's mouth gaped open. 'Cool, isn't it?' I was almost preening, enjoying being one-up on her. For once.

For some reason, I was feeling the necessity to paint the Miramar in as good a light as I could. Maybe Ellie would forget about her mission to save me from terrors unknown and calm down long enough for us to enjoy our visit.

It didn't work.

'Maids and room service won't save your skin when trouble comes hunting for you, AJ. And it's coming. The cards said so.' Ellie folded her arms defiantly and I sighed. There was no moving this woman when she had her mind made up.

'Ellie, nothing's going to happen. That body had nothing to do with me …' And that was as far as I got.

'Body? What body? Augusta Jerusha Burnette, you had better spill the beans and you'd better make it snappy!' Ellie's voice had elevated to such a degree that I was afraid someone would call the front desk and complain. I made a shushing motion at her and sank onto the couch. The food would have to wait.

'Look, we had a lost child this morning, I mean yesterday morning ...' Another squeal, more flapping of hands, this time accompanied by eye rolling. Ellie was the Master of Eye Rolling, a gift she'd perfected in our teens, and this time she almost outdid herself.

I raised my hand. 'If you insist on interrupting me, Ellie, I'm going straight back to bed. Can you be quiet long enough for me to talk?' I stared at her with my best 'angry mom' imitation. It worked. Ellie nodded meekly, settling back onto the couch next to me.

'Like I was saying, we had a lost child, a six-year-old girl who apparently sleepwalks. I have no idea where they found her, but I do know they discovered a body, a man, somewhere nearby. We, the employees, spent most of the morning talking to some detectives.'

Here an errant dimple wormed its way into my memory and I blushed. Ellie narrowed her eyes. I would be interrogated the first chance she got.

'And after dinner, we had a dance out on one of the side patios and the keyboard player was electrocuted and died. That's all. I can't imagine why your cards would think I was the one in danger.' I stopped to take a breath.

Ellie stared at me. I could almost hear the windmills of her mind turning furiously in a wave of curiosity. Finally she spoke, stretching her back into the luxurious cushions and plopping her feet onto the coffee table.

'I'll take coffee and a croissant or two, as long as you're ordering, AJ. I can't think on an empty stomach.' Ellie looked at me expectantly. 'Well? Are you or aren't you?'

'Fine,' I grumbled. Sometimes I could kick myself for the things I offer to do. I cringed when I thought of the kitchen staff. I'm sure they thought that Emmy had hired an adolescent bottomless pit instead of a grown-up assistant concierge. Oh, well. I might as well take advantage of it and get myself something as well. And not cookies, AJ, I scolded myself.

I placed an order for croissants, scrambled eggs, and coffee, feeling a mite foolish but delighted when the voice on the other end said, 'And will you want cookies as well, Ms Burnette?'

Well, why not? Life's too short and all that. 'Sure. Send whatever you have.' I replaced the phone with a grin on my face.

It wasn't such a bad thing, having folks around who knew what I liked. Too bad David hadn't been like that. His conversations tended to be one-sided, now that I thought about it, and rarely did we do what I wanted. A smiling Detective Baird popped into my mind and I could feel the tell-tale flush creeping up my neck. I'll bet he'd be game to try something if I suggested it. And *that* particular little thought made me blush even more, and Ellie's radar homed in on me.

'So.' She stared me down with laser-like intensity. 'What is it you need to tell me, AJ?' Damn her perceptive antenna. That was more than likely the reason she'd scooted on down here so fast to begin with. Her cards had probably already ratted me out.

'It's absolutely nothing, Ellie.' I knew my face was still red and tried to sound as if I truly didn't care. I forced steel into my voice and returned her stare with an icy one of my own. It didn't work.

Now it was Ellie's turn to snort scornfully. 'That's not what the cards, said, AJ.'

I could have laughed aloud. Ellie is so predictable.

'Ellie,' I began in a soothing tone, not wanting to risk

another blow-up. 'I've only just decided to break it off with David and I'm definitely not on the market at this moment. Besides, most men aren't interested in fair play anyway and I'm pretty sure that Detective Dimple would ...'

I caught myself and stopped talking abruptly. Ellie's eyes, which had opened wider at the mention of David's demise in my life, suddenly stretched so far I fully expected to see an eyeball or two roll down her cheeks.

'Detective *Dimple?* Is that his name? Oh, my goodness!'

Ellie's laugh, which at this time of the morning was slightly cackle-ish, cannoned across the room and resounded off of the walls. I glared at her, my lips folded as tight as my arms as I waited for the merriment to subside.

We Were Not Amused.

Wiping her eyes and gasping for air – which I think was just for effect and not entirely real – Ellie swung around on the couch, crossing her legs and facing me directly.

'Detective Dimple,' she said in that tone I knew so well, the one that said, *Hmm, AJ – here's material I can work with.*

I spluttered, bouncing to my feet and stomping out to the kitchen. I needed something to do with my hands or I was afraid I'd throttle her, adding one more to the body count at the Miramar.

'That's not his name,' I threw over my shoulder. 'It's Detective Baird, and he talked to me twice yesterday, nothing exciting. In fact, I think that he thinks that I did it.' I began to heat water for tea, completely forgetting the tray I'd ordered.

'He couldn't possibly,' Ellie objected, following me in to the kitchen. She perched on one of the chairs that bookended the small table, clearly expecting me to go on. I would be danged if I would, though; I was still smarting from the 'Detective Dimple' episode.

'Look, AJ,' Ellie said when she finally figured out that I wasn't going to be forthcoming with any more juicy tidbits about the day before. 'I can't imagine anyone would really consider you a suspect in anything, except maybe in making bad decisions.'

'And what, exactly, does that mean?' I demanded. 'If you're talking about me coming to the Miramar, I seem to recall that *someone* ...' here I shot her a poisonous glare '... actually encouraged me to do this.'

'No, of course not,' she impatiently brushed my ire aside. 'I was talking about David. You seem to have sorted that out already, though, so that's OK. I was talking about your detective.'

'He's not *my* detective,' I replied, teeth gritted. I dumped way too many tea bags into the hot water just as a timid knock sounded on the front door.

I went to answer the door, glad for the interruption. I mean it – I adore my cousin, I really do, but sometimes I'd like to wring her neck. That's family for you, I guess.

The same little maid from yesterday stood there, puffy eyes evidence of her weariness. As I took the tray from her, though, I could see signs of tears. And something else I couldn't quite put my finger on. Was it guilt? Anger?

'Hey, what's wrong, Maria?' I asked with a hasty glance at her name badge. I set the tray down and went back to the door where she still stood, hands clutched together and tears starting down her face.

'Miguel,' she managed to get out before a wave of sobs shook her. I drew her into the room, shutting the door behind us. Ellie, her eyes back to Kewpie-doll width, stayed frozen in her chair. It was up to me, I guessed, to calm Maria down enough to open up and to get Ellie's ability to talk restored. Such was the life of an assistance concierge.

I led Maria to the couch, motioning Ellie to come join us. I shot her a warning look, knowing that Ellie most likely would want to 'read' Maria. I didn't need it to get out that I dabbled in the dark arts; it was already bad enough to have a reputation as a non-stop eater.

'Oh yes – this is Ellie, my cousin. She's paid me a surprise visit, all the way from our home town. Checking I'm OK,' I explained.

'So tell us what's wrong,' I said in my gentlest voice. I sat on the edge of the table in front of the weeping girl, patiently waiting for her to compose herself.

Wiping her eyes with the back of her hands, Maria looked up at me. I was startled to see the abject misery on her face, and began to think there must have been something more than just a fellow employee relationship going on between them. I was right, as it turned out.

'Miguel,' Maria began, looking back and forth between me and Ellie. 'He's my brother. *Was* my brother.' A new round of sobs shook her slight shoulders.

My earlier suspicion concerning Emmy and Miguel reared its ugly head and I gave a small shiver. Something was undeniably wrong at the Miramar.

Chapter Eight

My eyes met Ellie's across Maria's bowed form and I shrugged. I couldn't let on that I suspected something, and I refused to give Ellie fuel for her inquisitive mind. She did that on her own just fine.

I went in search of tissues. Our food was getting cold and I was suddenly hungry, in spite of the early hour. I figured we could eat while Maria talked, if she still wanted to.

Walking back into the living room, I saw that Ellie had scooted over closer to Maria and had placed an arm around her shoulders, murmuring quietly in her ear. Maria seemed calmer, and give Ellie credit; she does have a gift for talking folks off the ledge. She also tends to use such moments to her advantage, in my experience.

'Ah, Ellie,' I said, careful to not break whatever spell she was weaving but not wanting to give her a chance to whip out the ever-present cards. 'Why don't you take the tray to the table? You might as well eat while it's hot. Maria, you're welcome to stay and talk if you'd like.' I stood by the couch, looking down at the two with what I hoped was an encouraging smile fixed on my face. My stomach gave a loud rumble and I grimaced. My body could be such a traitor at times.

'It sounds like you're the one who needs to eat, AJ.' Ellie grinned up at me, standing to her feet. 'And besides, Maria has consented to let me read for her.'

I started to protest, but Ellie held up her hand.

'She agrees with me that the police probably need as much help as we can give them. Besides, I may be able to identify a person of interest for them.' She looked smugly at me, daring me to object.

Put that way, I'd sound like a spoilsport if I protested; after all, I wanted the killer caught as well, didn't I? I sighed. Ellie certainly knew how to turn the tables on me.

'Look, Ellie. We don't even know if Miguel was killed. For all we know, that was an accident. I mean, it was tragic, yeah, but murder? I think that's stretching things a bit.' I could play verbal volleyball as well as Ellie, if not better. After all, I'd perfected my game against hers years ago.

'It was no accident!' Maria surprised me with an eruption of emotion – Ellie and I forgot our sparring and turned to face her. Her face was contorted with the anger she was feeling, and I took an involuntary step back from her furious words.

Ellie reached over to pat Maria's arm, but the girl jerked away. I could almost see the steam venting from her ears as she sat there, breathing heavily and staring daggers at me.

'Maria, I'm sure the police ...' I began but got no further.

'The police! They know nothing! I tried to tell them about things and they would not listen to me.' Maria was wound up as tightly as an eight-day clock. 'Wait,' I interrupted. 'What things do you mean? About Miguel?'

'Yes! I saw her do it, but they take no notice. Just a maid, they think,' she finished, spitting out the words scornfully, tossing her head. She sat back against the sofa's cushions, suddenly winding down. Tears began to fill her large dark eyes again. 'If they will not listen, then she can read the cards,' she said with a quaver, gesturing toward Ellie. 'Maybe she can tell us who killed my brother.'

I refused to look at my cousin. It was too early in the day to deal with an insufferable Ellie.

I sighed. I seemed to be doing quite a bit of that already this morning. My stomach grumbled, a bit more loudly this time. I needed to eat something if I was to handle Maria and Ellie.

'Fine,' I agreed ungraciously. 'I need to eat first, and Ellie, you might as well eat something, too. Maria?' I said, gesturing at the tray.

She waved me away. 'No, thank you. I am not hungry. You eat, then Miss Ellie will tell us who did this to Miguel.'

She settled back onto the couch with determination on her face. She had found a champion in Ellie, and my cousin was eating it up. I still wouldn't look at her, but I could feel her preening as she filled a plate with scrambled eggs and a croissant. Ellie was never going to let me forget this one.

We ate in silence for the most part, making inconsequential conversation about news from back home (I'd only been gone a little over a day but Ellie acted like it had been a week) and the day's plans. Finally I could stall no longer, having all but scraped the finish from the plate in front of me.

'Ellie, if you're going to read for Maria, do it quick. She probably needs to get back.' I figured if I made it sound like Maria was being timed, Ellie might not be so keen to do this. She was always saying that she couldn't force information from the cards if the 'spirits weren't listening' anyway. Maybe giving said spirits a time limit would drive them away completely.

So much for *that* little ploy. Ellie smiled benevolently at Maria, who sat up expectantly as if she thought Ellie would transform before her eyes into something magical and wave a wand over all her troubles. I rolled my eyes;

I'm skeptical about Ellie's so-called talents and I wasn't afraid to show her.

Refusing to be a part of Ellie's dog and pony show, I left them to it while I went to take a shower. My two cups of coffee were kicking in and I needed to get my morning started. I'd planned on being in the main lobby by eight anyway, and it looked like I'd be there with plenty of time to spare. Besides, I was certain Emmy would want to get an early start since work seemed to be a panacea for her.

The water was relaxing and I let it run over my shoulders and neck for a while. I figured Ellie would need about twenty minutes, start to finish, for her little bag of tricks; I could be showered, dried, and dressed by then, ready to face both Maria and the day.

When I walked back into the living room, I was surprised to find it empty. I was stumped: where in the world could Ellie and Maria have gotten to? It wasn't like the Miramar had a special room for card readings and crystal balls. I thought for a moment and then decided to head down toward the kitchen. Maybe Maria had already gone back there and would be able to tell me where Ellie had gone.

The sight that met my eyes, when I finally found the large, industrially equipped kitchen, nearly stopped me dead in my tracks. My cousin was holding court in a most regal Ellie-like manner, cards spread out across a stainless steel counter and surrounded by a hushed crowd of kitchen staff, Maria at the front.

'Ellie!' I exclaimed, breaking the near-reverential silence. 'What in heaven's name are you doing?'

All heads swiveled in my direction, eyes wide as though I had just sprouted a pair of horns and a tail. Ellie kept her head down, flipping cards and muttering to herself. She acted as though she hadn't heard me. Irritation bubbled up inside me; I didn't need to lose my newly landed job over something like this. I marched over to where she stood, stopping just short of sweeping the entire mess onto the polished floor.

Ellie still didn't look up, but instead raised one hand in a 'Stop' sign. I did as instructed. I really do hate confrontations.

Hesitating just a moment, I leant forward and hissed just loud enough for her to hear me, 'Ellie! Whatever it is you think you're doing, stop it right now! Number one, you're going to get me fired. And number two, we don't even know if Miguel was murdered or not. Pack it up and let's get out of here.'

I'd gotten her attention. 'AJ, would you just chill? I'm almost done and I think I know what happened. Besides, I promised Maria that I'd help.' With that she continued flipping the cards, finally stopping with a loud, 'Aha!'

I shook my head, half-disgusted at her theatrics. Only Ellie could make card reading seem like a Broadway show.

'What do you see, Miss?' Maria eagerly questioned Ellie as the rest of the folks surged forward to see how the cards were laid out. In spite of myself, I moved closer as well, taking a look at the various figures galloping, hanging, and grinning on the cards' surfaces. I could make neither head nor tail of them, and frankly, I had no wish to. It was nothing but a lot of mumbo-jumbo to me, but Ellie seemed to believe in the messages she claimed to get. As long as she wasn't making promises she couldn't deliver, I supposed it was OK.

A sudden flurry of action dropped me back into the present. The kitchen staff had vanished as if by magic, and I half-expected Ellie to have disappeared as well. Footsteps behind me caused me to turn, and I saw Emmy standing just inside the doorway, her face set, shoulders held stiffly. Something had her knickers in a twist, and I crossed my fingers that it wasn't Ellie. Or me, for that matter. I had no desire to go back home with my tail between my legs.

'AJ, you're up early.' Emmy Ruiz walked into the kitchen, her expression already harried despite the early hour. 'Detective Baird has called and tells me that he will be here around two to speak with you."

'With me?' I all but squeaked. 'What in the world does he want with me?'

'For that, you will need to see the detective,' Emmy said with a small smile.

I relaxed. She was just anxious over the on-going investigation, not mad at me. I gave a half-glance over my shoulder and saw that Ellie had evaporated as well, and that was probably a good thing. I wasn't sure how I'd explain her to Emmy anyway, and I certainly couldn't imagine justifying a card reading in the resort's kitchen. I looked back at Emmy, who was staring at me with an unreadable expression that instantly vanished when our eyes met.

'Let's get something to eat before our day starts and the handsome detective comes calling, shall we?' Emmy turned toward the door, stopping to see if I was following.

We made our way to the Palmetto Room, its tables beginning to fill with early-morning risers. Large coffee urns shone at each end of a long serving table, bracketing platters of croissants, fruit, and pastries, alongside steaming dishes of scrambled eggs and bacon. In spite of the fact that I'd already eaten that morning, my stomach began its familiar refrain. I really needed to get that under control pronto, otherwise I'd soon be rolling around the Miramar like an unwieldy beach ball.

That particular thought didn't stop me from filling a plate with food, although I did manage to get some fruit on there as well. With self-righteous satisfaction, I nibbled at pineapple and mango before diving into the eggs and bacon that took up a large portion of my plate. Ah. Now this was the way to begin a day, I told myself. Especially

when the day would hold a visit from a certain detective whose mere presence could send me into a dither.
    A girl needs her strength, after all.

Chapter Nine

True to his word, Detective Baird *sans* Fischer appeared in the main lobby of the Miramar at precisely two o'clock. Emmy had departed to parts unknown to take care of resort business, leaving me to fend for myself; even Ellie had done a disappearing act. I steeled my mind; I would not be taken in by his devastating charm once again.

That resolution lasted exactly three seconds. Spotting me across the room, Detective Baird let go with a barrage of dimples, instantly turning my knees to putty and my mind to mush. Apparently that second breakfast had not done its job.

I could see Detective Baird had ditched his usual costume for jeans and a button-down shirt, tucked into a waistband that emphasized his slim build. He looked more like an executive enjoying a day off for golf, or a casual lunch, instead of an officer knee-deep in a murder investigation. In short, he was lookin' mighty good.

'Concentrate, AJ, concentrate,' I muttered to myself, trying hard not to let my eyes wander in places they had no business going. If I wasn't careful, I'd find myself confessing to the crime just to keep him around for a while.

He joined me at Emmy's desk. I'd retreated to the business side to keep myself – to keep myself what? Protected? I almost got the giggles as I had a sudden image of me as 'damsel in distress', cowering behind the computer tower as a devastatingly handsome rogue that looked vaguely like Detective Baird leaned over me.

Hmm. Maybe that wasn't such a bad idea after all.

'Good afternoon, Ms Burnette,' he said easily as he slipped his well-filled jeans into the chair next to the desk. 'What, no coffee?'

He looked around the room as if a carafe might magically appear, provided he searched hard enough. I did a mini eye roll; I can take a hint. I reached for the phone and ordered a plate of cookies as well as two large coffees. Besides, I told myself, I was going to do that anyway. I was definitely in need of a dose of equilibrium-restoring sugar.

Cookies and coffee delivered, I sat back and waited for him to tell me what he'd come about. Instead, to my consternation, he chatted about the weather ('Really nice today. Do you sail?'), the Miramar in general ('These are really good cookies.'), and why I took the job here ('What does San Blanco have that your hometown doesn't?'). That last question gave me pause: what *did* San Blanco have over the place I grew up in? Besides a gorgeous beach, a fabulous job, and him? Exactly nothing. I didn't share this thought with him, though.

Draining his coffee and brushing the crumbs of his third cookie from his jeans, Detective Baird finally settled into official mode, reaching over to retrieve the clipboard and pen he had laid on the floor beside his chair. My heart rate picked up a bit; I wasn't certain if it was from the impending questions or the sight of his strongly muscled arms. Either way, I was feeling rattled.

'So,' he began, tapping the end of his pen against the paper. 'What was your day like yesterday? Begin with the earliest thing you can remember and take it from there.'

He looked at me expectantly, and I just stared back. Was he serious?

'Well, I had breakfast in the Palmetto Room, helped Emmy get Mrs Reilly calmed down –'

'The mother of the lost girl, I take it?' he interrupted. I

nodded.

'Then I got my things settled in my room, had lunch there, and went out to help Emmy with a group of scrapbookers who were in town for a convention.' I paused, looking out the large window opposite me. I could see someone at work on the herbaceous borders lining the drive. That reminded me about Emmy and her walk past those same flower beds.

'Oh, and I covered the front desk when Emmy went to check on the sound system. That was about four-ish, I think. That's about it, aside from dinner and the dance.'

I stopped talking, waiting for direction. Detective Baird's head was down as he wrote his notes with an easy script, giving me a great view of his profile. Absolutely gorgeous, I decided, trying to think of something to say that would bring that ravaging dimple out of hiding. No, that was a bad idea, I reminded myself. I didn't want to deal with a blushing episode again.

I've never been a delicate girl, always a bit ungainly, and I've never managed to learn the art of girlie ploys. When I'm embarrassed, I tend to go a mottled reddish-pink, looking more like a sunburn victim than a reticent young woman twirling a parasol or fluttering a fan – you know, like one of those ditzy gals in old movies.

I realized he was waiting for an answer to some question that I had totally spaced, and I could feel the dreaded mottling beginning to creep up my neck. Fabulous. And I hadn't even had the pleasure of observing that dimple peek out, to make the blush worth it.

Detective Baird was still waiting for my answer, so I sheepishly admitted that I hadn't heard a word he'd said. His blue eyes twinkled at me, making me feel like he'd read my mind, and I did that crazy hot-cold thing that seemed to happen whenever he was around. Good thing I was sitting down already; I might've bit the dust.

'No, I didn't actually *see* Emmy check the sound

equipment. That's just what she told me.' I looked intently at him, trying to read meaning behind his question concerning Emmy's whereabouts. I had no earthly idea why he'd go down that road; so distressed had Emmy been, I knew she couldn't possibly have had anything to do with Miguel's death.

Or could she? A recollection popped into my mind and I remembered that peculiar look on her face when the accident had happened. That had been odd, no doubt about it. But murderous? I couldn't say.

Detective Baird clicked the pen shut, signifying the end of our conversation. I was disappointed; it hadn't lasted nearly long enough, from my point of view, and I knew that it showed on my face. I have never been able to file my feelings away as neatly as others can. I could see right away my message had been sent and received, loud and clear. Great. That was all I needed; to come across as a kid with a crush.

He laughed, flashing that amazing smile that sent a bolt of something tingly racing down my spine.

'I need to talk to some of the kitchen staff, AJ. Care to walk over there with me?'

Oh, wonder of wonders! He'd used my name. This sent my temperature fluctuating again; I was beginning to feel like a water tap, switching back and forth from hot to cold and back to boiling in a matter of seconds. Or maybe I was coming down with some tropical disease. Either way, I was walking on a cloud.

'Sure, no problem,' I replied, trying to sound casual, as though strolling with the world's handsomest man was an everyday occurrence.

Miraculously, I was able to put one foot in front of the other all the way through the maze of corridors. The kitchen, situated near the middle back portion of the resort, had two entrances. I chose to go through the one I'd used that morning when I was looking for Ellie. I figured I'd be able to find at least a handful of staff there, and I would keep an eye out for Maria. After what she'd said in my room that morning, I wanted Detective Baird to talk to her before he left.

I led the way into the kitchen. We were in luck: Maria was standing with her back to us, putting a tray together for a room service delivery. I walked over to her and tapped her on the shoulder, startling her and nearly sending her into orbit. I caught the tray just as it tipped over the counter's edge. No need to waste those luscious cookies.

I introduced Detective Baird to the timid girl, backing quietly out of the kitchen. I figured she'd be more likely to talk without an audience.

I spent the next hour or so working on a project Emmy had left for me, looking up every time someone walked into the lobby. I was hoping to see a certain pair of jeans strolling into view. And I had to admit that I was curious as to who he was talking to. It would seem that the police department considered Miguel's death something other than an accident.

I found myself wondering if Emmy knew that.

Sadly, the afternoon passed without another glimpse of Detective Baird. For that matter, I'd seen neither hide nor hair of Emmy. I sat for a moment, thinking, trying to decide if I should try to find her or look for something else to do. I decided not to do either, heading to my room instead to see if Ellie was still here or had flown the coop. I half-hoped I'd find an empty suite, but experience told me Ellie would still be there, ensconced on my couch, making herself right at home.

I was right. Ellie lay asleep, stretched out on the couch, making snorting noises and looking like she could sleep for hours. I stood just inside the door for a minute, watching her and grinning as I recalled the crazy scrapes we'd gotten into as kids. In a town the size of ours, there was little chance of having secrets or getting away with anything, but Ellie and I had managed to fly under the radar, creating mischief and having a blast.

Here at the Miramar, though, flying under the radar probably wasn't a great idea. I would need to let the powers that be understand that she was here to act as bodyguard and lookout for yours truly. *And* to take advantage of the resort's amenities, if I knew my cousin.

I managed to restrain myself from pouring water on her like she used to do to me whenever I spent the night at her house. It would not do to get her wound up; I knew she still had an impish streak, and revenge was her middle name. I contented myself with a quick shake of her shoulder.

'Hey, AJ,' she said sleepily, propping herself up on her elbows. 'What time is it?' She laid back down, flinging one arm across her face to block out the late afternoon light.

'Just past five,' I replied, walking into the kitchen and opening the fridge. Since there was absolutely nothing in there, it was clearly out of habit. I closed the door and leaned back on the counter.

'How about a quick walk before dinner?' I suggested, checking my watch. We'd have just enough time for a turn around the resort before the Palmetto Room would be opened. I intended to be in the first crowd of folks so I'd have time to chat with Emmy.

I still hadn't heard from her and I was getting anxious. I hoped she was OK, considering the bad news about Miguel and the suspicions that surrounded his demise. She was so protective of the Miramar and its reputation and something like a murder inquiry could be devastating.

'This place is incredible!' Ellie stood near the path that led to the beach, looking back at the resort with one hand protecting her eyes from the sun.

I felt a proprietary pride, nodding in agreement. 'Yeah,

it sure is. I picked a winner, that's for sure.'
Ellie turned to look at me. 'So, what're your plans, AJ? Do you mean to stay, or will you be coming back to the nest?'
I snorted. 'Not any time soon. I like it here, and I couldn't find a job like this back home if I looked for a hundred years.' And so far, Emmy hadn't asked to me to fetch her dry-cleaning, so that made it an even better gig in my book.
I took a long look at the Miramar. The buildings spread out proudly across the beachfront, giving no hint of the tragedy of the day before. I earnestly hoped that nothing else would happen to spoil its peaceful ambiance.

Chapter Ten

When dinner came and went, and still there was no sign of Emmy, I began to get really worried. I didn't think anything had happened to her; rather, I was beginning to suspect that she was avoiding people in general. Why, I couldn't say, but it still didn't look good for the Miramar's most public of employees.

Ellie and I lingered over our well-filled plates, reminiscing and laughing so hard that others began to stare. A few of the staff still in the Palmetto Room stifled grins of their own whenever they passed our table; the Miramar, after all, had a reputation to uphold.

Our family is a great one for good times and fun for all. Ellie and I have always been the resident gigglers; whenever we two get started, there's no stopping us, and everything is grounds for merriment. Finally, though, sated with food and laughter, we staggered to our feet and headed out into a perfect balmy evening.

We began to stroll toward the beach, the sound of the waves and the call of the seagulls a beacon, urging a visit to the water's edge. I have to admit that this was the biggest draw for me when I applied for the job; the idea of living practically beachside intrigued this mountain girl to no end.

We paused by an outcrop of rocks, some of them perfect for sitting and staring at the ocean. I sat on the largest, Ellie on the one just below. We rested silently for a few minutes, taking in the tranquility of our surroundings. The beach was deserted, except for a few seagulls tussling over something buried in the sand, so we had it to ourselves.

'Ellie,' I said abruptly, leaning forward. 'I never asked you about your card reading this morning, the one you did for Maria. You said something about knowing who had done it. What was *that* all about?'

Ellie kept her face forward, the fading light of sunset defining the edges of her silhouette. 'I saw something that bothered me, AJ,' she answered quietly.

'I did, too: I saw my cousin practically turning the Miramar's kitchen into a carnival sideshow.' I gave her a friendly poke in the back, but she didn't take the bait. Ellie must've been really rattled, even more than I'd thought.

'I'm afraid it's not over yet,' she said, her voice almost inaudible as she stared out over the waves. 'Not by a long shot.'

I stayed silent. What could I say to that? Besides, I'd begun to get the heebie-jeebies as well, especially since Emmy seemed to have gone AWOL from the resort.

Eventually we stood to leave, darkness and dampness encouraging us to scoot back to the Miramar. Besides, I needed to do the last check of the night at the desk, making sure that all guests were happy, no one wanting for anything.

As we began to pick our way across the rocks and head toward the path, a loud squawking arose behind us. Ellie and I turned to look, but it was just dark enough to keep us from getting a clear view. I looked at her and shrugged.

'Do we need to check it out? It's probably just seagulls fighting over someone's leftovers.' I didn't have any real wish to walk across the wet sand, but Ellie turned and started moving in the direction of the avian fracas.

The closer we got to the large seabirds, the more we could see what it was they were fussing over. Something large and dark lay near the water's edge, half in the water and moving gently in the current. Apparently someone had left behind one of the Miramar's large beach blankets; available at the concierge's desk, these could get quite heavy when wet. I grimaced. I had no desire to cart it all the way back to the resort, dripping and dragging against my legs. It would just have to stay there until I could get someone a little stronger than me to retrieve it.

Ellie began walking more quickly, her presence scattering the birds at the periphery of the feathered mob. They settled back on the sand a few feet away, scolding her as she advanced on the others. With a mad flapping of wings and coarse cries, the remainder of the gulls took flight, wheeling above us and screeching their displeasure. I didn't blame them: I hate it when someone interferes in my life, too.

I should have known at once that something was amiss by Ellie's stance. She was completely still, head down and focused on the blanket. As I watched, she bent her knees, leaning in closer for a better look. It's a good thing I'd moved up behind her – I caught her as she slumped sideways onto the sand, choking and crying at the same time.

We'd found Emmy.

I think I was the one who alerted the resort's security, stumbling into the main lobby and scaring the few guests who'd congregated in front of the small fire burning in the stone fireplace. Someone guided me to a chair and got me a glass of water, murmuring soothing words as they patted my shoulders and waited for help to arrive. I had no idea where Ellie was; for all I knew, she was still on the beach, keeping a macabre vigil over Emmy's battered body.

I really shouldn't have been in the least surprised to see the familiar figures of Detectives Baird and Fischer as they strode up the resort's front walkway and into the lobby. I was beginning to feel like the resort albatross, courting disaster and bringing bad luck wherever I went. Logically, I knew none of this was my fault, but really! What was a girl to think with this many bodies piling up in such a short amount of time?

I'd sufficiently recovered enough by this time to look around for Ellie, craning my neck to see if she had made it back to the resort. I finally spotted her sitting near the entrance to the main corridor, being comforted by Maria and another gal from the kitchen staff. Bad news sure grew wings at the Miramar, I was discovering.

'So, Ms Burnette,' a familiar voice intoned. I looked up to see Detective Fischer bearing down on me, notebook in one hand and pen in the other. I felt a stab of disappointment, expecting Detective Baird to be the one who spoke with me. Oh, well: I didn't own the man. I sure wanted to, though.

I met the detective's eyes, a flat blue compared to the dazzling pair of his partner. I was tired, and I wanted to get the questioning over and done with. I took a calming breath in, willing myself to focus.

'Yes, Detective?' I answered. I wasn't going to offer anything this time around; he'd have to pull it out of me piecemeal.

'I just need a few basics,' he began. I managed to keep myself from rolling my eyes; wasn't that what they all said, right before a big interrogation?

'When did you last see Esmeralda Ruiz?' He had to check his notes for the name, which surprised me. I figured that by now, he and Detective Baird knew everyone and everything connected to the ill-fated Miramar.

'I saw her this morning, about 6-ish, in the kitchen,' I offered, watching him scribble the information into his notebook.

He looked up at me. 'OK. Did you see her last night?'

'Well, yes, right before you let us go when ...' My voice trailed off. I really didn't want to talk to him about Miguel. I could still see his body as it jerked and sparked on the bandstand, and it was not a good memory at all.

He nodded. I guess that jived with his notes.

'Right, that's it for now, Ms Burnette. Don't go anywhere; we may need to ask you a few more questions, OK?' With that, he strode off in the direction of his partner, who was still leaning over Ellie and talking to her.

As if I had anywhere *to* go, I thought grimly. I was beginning to rethink this whole job-at-a-resort gig, though. Somehow, it hadn't turned out like I thought it would.

The few guests who'd remained in the lobby started drifting off to various destinations, huddling together and looking warily around as though they expected to see a mad killer running loose. I shuddered. For all I knew, there *was* a killer somewhere nearby. I just prayed that I stayed out of his – or her – crosshairs.

I waited where I was for a while, contemplating a call for my go-to sugar fix and some strong tea. I didn't have the energy to get up and walk to the nearest phone, though. Everything that had happened since I'd arrived had worn me out. I felt like one of the limp dishrags drying in the kitchen.

The kitchen! I flashed back to the sight of kitchen staff huddled around Ellie in intense silence, waiting to hear what my cousin would say. I glanced over to where Ellie sat, Maria still hovering over her like a concerned mother hen guarding an injured chick. Making up my mind, I rose to my feet and headed in their direction.

Ellie's eyes were swollen, her face streaked with tears and sand. She must've gotten awfully close to Emmy's body as it lay in the surf, moving gently in the water. I groaned; my aunt was going to hold this over my head for as long as I lived.

'Hey, Ellie,' I said gently, reaching over to wipe some of the grit from her cheeks. 'It's OK, I promise.' I had no idea if it would be OK or not but I had to say something. I glanced up at Maria who stood there with wide eyes.

'Could you get us some hot tea, Maria? And maybe something to munch on? Get enough for the three of us.' She nodded and left, giving Ellie a final pat on the shoulder.

With Maria off on her errand, I squatted down next to Ellie, looking up into her face. She looked absolutely done in, worse even than when we'd gotten stuck in the middle of a stream that had risen quicker than we'd expected. We'd been about eight years old, stranded on a sandbar and bellowing for our mamas. When at last our fathers found us, huddled together, shivering and crying, we'd both been on the verge of hysterics.

Ellie seemed to have left me, moving somewhere near the polar opposite of her earlier hysteria, sitting in stunned silence and not speaking. I was worried, wondering if I should call for help. It's safe to say that I was startled when she finally spoke, her voice low and gravelly from weeping.

'I knew something would happen and it has. I could have prevented this, AJ.' With that, she began to weep again, large tears slipping from her eyes and sliding down her face. I reached up and held her in my arms, rocking her slightly back and forth, trying to give her comfort. I felt my own eyes begin to sting. Keeping Ellie with me no longer seemed like such a great idea.

As we sat drinking the tea that Maria brought, I turned the events of the day over and over in my head. I knew there had to be a connection between the three deaths, but what it was, for the life of me, I couldn't see. I prayed with all my heart that this would end soon; I didn't want to see one more body as long as I lived.

Chapter Eleven

To my great disappointment, Detective Baird never came back. I suppose he went down to the beach, looking for clues and all that other jazz that detectives do whenever a suspicious death occurs. Emmy's death, in my book, was certainly suspicious. What I couldn't figure out was why someone would be out to get Emmy, would be so angry that they'd feel the need to get rid of her. It certainly was strange. But the Miramar was fast becoming a magnet for strange occurrences.

I put Ellie to sleep in my bed, opting to take the couch and be near the phone in case something else happened during the night. I could hear her tossing and muttering occasionally, but she stayed asleep for the most part and awakened me around seven the following morning.

I ordered breakfast for us, not wanting to face the rest of the staff just then. It had occurred to me some time during the night that I was now 'acting' concierge. I'd need to double-check with the resort manager – I'd met him briefly on that very first day – and see what he wanted me to do. In the meantime, Ellie and I needed nourishment, and I needed to figure out what I would wear; I hadn't brought too many formal work clothes with me to San Blanco, having been assured by Emmy that the Miramar leaned toward casual. I'd seen how Emmy dressed, though, and I felt the need to emulate her. Maybe that would help me keep my newly crowned concierge head above water.

Someone new brought our breakfast tray, a young girl who

looked about ten. She was probably at least nineteen or so, but her slender build and shy stance gave her that childlike appearance. As quickly as she could, she handed me the tray and scooted down the corridor, heading, I guess, back to the kitchen. I briefly wondered where Maria was, then turned my attention to eating: per usual, I was starving or doing a good imitation of it.

The view from my bedroom window showed an early morning that was bright with just a touch of wispy clouds floating near the horizon, looking like flocks of seagulls floating on the waves. Regrettably, the clouds that reminded me of birds also brought back the memory of Emmy's body as it lay on the shore, the center of an avian squabble.

I was going to have to wash that visual from my mind if I was going to function.

I drew in a deep breath, leaning my forehead against the cool glass for a moment, corralling my thoughts, organizing the day. A shower was the first step, though, so I shut the blinds and turned to get ready for whatever adventure – hopefully of the happier variety – awaited me.

Ellie was still seated on the couch, sipping hot tea and staring off into space. I hoped she wasn't revisiting last night's calamity; even more, I hoped that she wasn't still blaming herself. Cards or not, she couldn't have possibly foreseen the tragedy of Emmy's death. On second thoughts, it might have been better if she had: we might not have had to find Emmy the way we did.

With a promise to join me in the lobby as soon as she'd showered and dressed, Ellie stood to her feet and hugged me. 'AJ, stay safe out there. This place gives me the creeps, room service or not. I'll come find you as soon as I can.' She really did look worried.

I laughed, although it came out sounding a little strangled – which, come to think of it, is not such a good descriptor, considering all the deaths around here.

Anyway, it was good to be fussed over, although I would've preferred different circumstances. I wasn't too anxious, though; I highly doubted the Miramar Murderer (as I'd privately dubbed him) would strike in broad daylight.

Stanley West, the resort's general manager, was waiting at Emmy's desk. Actually, he was pacing up and down the lobby, stopping every so often to glance out of the window as though expecting something else to happen. He had the appearance of someone whose nerves were on edge, and I couldn't say that I blamed him one iota. Mine would be, too, if I had to deal with staff, menus, activities, *and* a killer.

'AJ, there you are! I was just debating whether or not to call your suite. In fact, I wasn't even sure you'd stick around after all this.' Stan waved his arms expansively. I guessed that he'd never had to deal with anything more than a miffed guest or a no-show employee before, so this must have been close to pure catastrophe in his book.

This entire situation was probably more of a draw than he knew. I had a hunch that, before long, folks would be clamoring for a room at the Miramar: those who liked an amateur ghost hunt, those who were drawn to the macabre, and those who just enjoyed a good scare. Emmy's death, as unfortunate and untimely as it was, could serve as a catalyst in reinforcing the Miramar's reputation as the place to be. That, I was fairly certain, was something she would have been proud of, as weird as it sounded.

'Hey, Stan,' I said, aiming for 'casual happy' to match my khaki pants and linen shirt. It wouldn't do to seem rattled; I had a feeling that I would be called upon to play the part of Emmy today. 'I got here as soon as I could. Just let me know what you need me to do.' I smiled at him as I headed for Emmy's desk. Flipping on the computer's power switch and the little desk lamp, I sat down, folding my hands and trying to project efficiency and control *à la*

Esmeralda Ruiz.

Stan ran both hands through his hair, creating little tufts that stood up over his ears. I had to hide a smile; he looked like one of the characters from a children's puppet show, the kind that look like big fuzzy tennis balls with mouths.

'I think that if we can just make it through today, we'll be OK. Detective Bread told me he'd be back later this morning for a few more interviews.'

I smiled, not bothering to camouflage my amusement this time. 'Do you mean Detective *Baird?*'

Stan stopped his pacing and looked at me like I'd sprouted horns. 'That's what I just said. Anyway,' he added, resuming his fidgety movements, 'We should be fixed for the weekend. Emmy had already lined up a few things that we'll go on with. Hopefully this will all blow over soon.'

That little phrase threw me for a loop. *This will all blow over soon?* He made it sound like the three deaths were inconveniences to his precious resort, which maybe they were, at least to him.

'Speaking of interviews,' I said, managing to sound composed, 'when will you start looking for a new concierge?'

Stan looked at me, eyebrows raised in surprise. 'I really hadn't thought that far ahead, AJ. I guess I just assumed that you'd want the job. You know. Move up a notch in the world.' His smile was magnanimous as though he'd just offered me the *crème de la crème* of jobs.

Oh, sure: who wouldn't want to work at a resort that could boast a resident killer? And you know what they say about assuming things. I'm not going to write it here, this being a family-friendly narrative. But you get the general idea. And I didn't want to be anything other than what I'd been hired for. I'd been able to tell from Emmy's stress levels that 'concierge' was just a fancy word that meant 'it's all on your back'.

I was saved from what might have been a regrettable retort by the appearance of my cousin. She looked more awake than she had when I'd left her earlier. In fact, she was practically emitting bursts of static electricity, and by the look on her face, she had Big News. The next order of business was to shoo Stan on his merry way and let Ellie spill the beans.

I managed to get rid of the jumpy resort manager by reassuring him that I wasn't going anywhere and that I would be able to handle two groups of guests arriving later that morning.

'I'd appreciate it if I had some help, though,' I said sweetly. My voice was as thick with honey as a beehive, and I hooked my arm through Ellie's, pulling her in close. 'My cousin just happened to be visiting the resort. She would be happy to assist me, if you'd OK it.' I could feel Ellie's arm stiffen but I held firm, that syrupy smile plastered on my face.

Stan gave Ellie the briefest of glances, nodding as he began walking away. 'Have her fill out the necessary papers, AJ, and make sure that HR gets them by the end of the day. Now, if that's all?'

I didn't have time to answer, even if I had wanted to. Stan was already strolling off to the next task, leaving me and an astounded Ellie to fend for ourselves. Whether we liked it or not, we'd just become a two-headed concierge for the Miramar.

'Well.' Ellie plopped down in to the chair I normally occupied, arms crossed and a stunned look on her face. Laser-like glare would probably be more accurate (as in 'stun gun'); I'd managed to enlist her help at the desk before she'd known what had hit her. Chalk one up for the ol' AJ, I thought with a grin. I hadn't lost my touch.

I checked the bookings for the day, noting that the two large tour parties were due to arrive before ten. Glancing at my wristwatch, I saw that we would have time to call out for the morning's cookies. I decided to have the kitchen put them into a napkin-lined basket instead of on the usual glass plate; Ellie was notoriously butter-fingered and I wasn't taking a chance.

The stock of brochures and area maps looked good, so I suggested to Ellie that we take a quick jaunt around the Miramar, making sure all was well with our guests. Besides, it didn't hurt to hobnob with the paying customers, as I had learned at the casino. The ones who felt noticed and loved were usually those who became repeat visitors. I didn't have Emmy's solicitous approach down yet, but I did know how to carry on a conversation without making a fool of myself. I figured that Ellie could tag along and feel for auras or whatever it was that she did. The sooner the Miramar Murderer was caught, the better.

Outside, the sky was a clear blue, something my pilot father would call a 'high sky', perfect for flying, birdwatching, and sunbathing. Standing in the sunshine and feeling the halcyon breezes blowing, it was difficult to imagine that this had been the scene of three deaths, all of which appeared suspicious. I glanced sideways at Ellie and saw she was staring off toward the beach. Not good, I thought, so I gave her a little poke in the ribcage.

'Hey, girl. None of that this morning.' I draped an arm across her shoulders and began walking, guiding her along the path.

Ellie remained quiet. Not a tense quiet, but 'lost in thought' type of quiet, contemplative. She'd give when she was ready, so I didn't push it. Besides, I needed to get the feel of my newly appointed position. I began to concentrate on the scene around me, nodding and smiling at the guests who sat with juice and coffee, enjoying the weather and the newspaper. I could get use to this, I thought. I was just beginning to feel like visiting royalty when I heard someone calling my name, and not in a casual, friendly voice, either. In fact, whoever it was sounded downright upset.

'Ms Burnette! Ms Burnette!' I turned to see Fernando and Maria running toward me, she waving something at me and him trying to keep up with the much younger and much quicker girl.

Ellie and I stopped in our tracks, opting to wait for the two to catch up. I knew what some of the guests were peeking surreptitiously around newspapers and from behind sunglasses, so I fixed what I hoped was a look of competence on my face and waited to hear whatever new disaster had just occurred.

Chapter Twelve

'Ms Burnette!' Maria was panting a bit as she reached Ellie and me, stopping mere inches before she mowed us down. 'Please take this.' She thrust something into my hands then turned to Ellie. 'Oh, Miss Ellie. There is so much trouble, just like you said to us. I have never seen so much trouble before.' And with that, she covered her face with her hands and burst into tears.

I left Ellie and Fernando to comfort Maria. I walked off a few paces, looking down at what Maria had handed to me. It was an envelope, crumpled from handling, and the name on the front was mine. Abrupt shivers marched up and down my spine like a holiday parade, sending my mind into a tailspin: I recognized the handwriting of Esmeralda Ruiz. The late Esmeralda Ruiz.

I turned around in time to see Ellie and Fernando walking back toward the Palmetto Room, Maria being led between them like a little child. I hesitated. Whatever was in the envelope, I wanted Ellie to see it as well, and I was just chicken enough not to open it until I was surrounded with the living. I made up my mind and followed them.

Ellie had commandeered a table near the back of the dining room, nearest the French doors and the sunlight. Fernando was up at the buffet table, getting coffee and a plateful of breakfast items. I watched approvingly as he spooned large amounts of sugar into one of the mugs and then carried it over to Maria. She still looked upset but took the coffee obediently, a good sign. I decided to follow Fernando's example and get my own mug-o'-sugar with a little coffee in it for color.

I slid into the empty chair next to Ellie. A few of the nosier guests were trying to watch us out of the corner of their eyes but gave up when I purposely leaned toward Maria, all but blocking their view. What is it about folks and their need for the salacious in life? We've grown into a society where everything is fodder for a reality show.

We sat quietly, sipping the hot drinks and letting the warmth fill us. Stress makes me shiver, and I could see that Maria was trembling slightly as well, the mug held tightly in two hands so she wouldn't drop it.

I fished the envelope from my pants pocket where I had shoved it unceremoniously. The others watched me with curiosity, Ellie because she had no idea what I was holding and the other two because they did. Holding my breath, I slipped my index finger under the flap and gently teased it open. I didn't need a nasty paper cut in addition to everything else.

It was a short letter, addressed to me – no surprise there, since it was my name on the envelope – and written in Emmy's careful, looping handwriting. I read it once, then again. What she said made no sense to me. Then again, I'd never had a letter from the dead before.

Ellie's eyebrows had ridden so far up her forehead that I almost couldn't see them. It was obvious she wanted to know what the letter said, so I handed it to her without comment, waiting for her to read it and make her own sense of it. And if she didn't get those eyebrows down quickly, they might become permanently attached to her hairline.

'Well.' Ellie slowly handed the letter back over, her eyes locked on mine. I took the missive, tucking it back into its envelope as carefully as if it had been a defused bomb. I guess it was, in its own way; the words Emmy had penned were as explosive as dynamite.

I nodded. 'I know. Crazy, isn't it?' I couldn't think of

anything else to say, and I certainly wasn't going to let Maria and Fernando know what it said. I did have a question for them, though.

'Where did you get this, Maria?' I waggled the letter in her direction. It might have more made sense to me if Emmy had left it at the front desk with directions to deliver it to me, but I had a sneaking suspicion that the front desk was not where Maria had gotten it.

Maria flushed, her eyes shifting from me to the letter and back again. It was if she needed to verify that yes, indeed, I had meant that particular letter.

'I got it from her room,' Maria finally whispered, her eyes now on the table. 'Please do not tell on me, Ms Burnette. I cannot lose my job.'

With that, tears began sliding from her eyes and falling onto the table. Fernando reached over and put a comforting arm around her, giving me a look that said something along the lines of 'you'd better not tell a soul'. I got the message loud and clear, and nodded briefly at him to show that I had. Satisfied, he turned his attention to the sobbing girl.

Ellie and I looked at each other. We'd need to show this to the police, that was for sure, but first I wanted to do some checking on my own. What Emmy had said flipped this entire thing on its ugly head, and I needed to see for myself if what she'd alleged was true. Call it a death wish, call it the Saddler gene for curiosity, call it whatever you will: I had a burning need to know the truth.

'Maria,' I began gently, reaching over to pat her hand. 'It's OK. I won't tell anyone where this came from. Promise.' *Unless I have to*, I added silently, mentally crossing my fingers for good measure.

She looked up at me, her large brown eyes rimmed in red, lashes clumped together with tears. 'Oh, *gracias*, Ms Burnette. Thank you. I know that I shouldn't have gone in there, but …' A fresh wave of sobs began to shake her thin shoulders, and she leaned into Fernando for support.

I looked at Ellie, trying to bombard her with my best ESP attempt. Actually, I'd never tried anything like that before, so any attempt was my best. And by the way Ellie stared back at me, she had no earthly idea what I was trying to transmit to her. Dang. I'd just have to say it out loud.

'Uh, Ellie, dear cuz. I think we need to check out the concierge desk, make sure that all's quiet on the Western Front.' My little shot at humor fell flat on its face. Ellie simply looked at me as though I'd lost the last of my marbles, and Maria kept crying, a little quieter now. Only Fernando seemed to have gotten my drift. He nodded at me.

'I will take Maria back to the kitchen, Ms Burnette,' he offered. 'She will be safe with me.' Tugging gently on Maria's arm, Fernando lifted her to her feet and they left the dining room together, Fernando's arm protectively holding her close.

Unlike Ellie, I certainly don't lay any claim to reading the future or anything, but I didn't need a crystal ball to tell me which way the wind was blowing in that scenario. At least someone would be happy. And Maria certainly deserved some happiness in her life.

Ellie and I walked back to the main lobby, taking the scenic route behind the Palmetto and across the large grassy lawn that encircled the resort like a green shawl. All *was* quiet on the Western Front, and I breathed a deep sigh of relief; I was just plain tired of dealing with drama every day.

Of course, that thought set off the built-in guilt alarm that my mother had honed at an early age. This 'so-called' drama was the result of three murders, and probably not high on the victims' lists of 'Things to Do While at the Miramar.' If I wasn't careful, I'd become as cavalier as Stan West.

The concierge desk, tucked back from the main portion of the lobby, provided some privacy and was as good a place as any to go over Emmy's letter before I had to make the call to Detective Baird (as if *that* would be a chore). I still couldn't quite get my head around her words, but she must've known what she was talking about. What really troubled me was that she could sense danger enough to cause her to write her thoughts down, and with my name on the envelope, this was a recent development. I shivered. Who at the Miramar could hate enough to kill three seemingly unrelated folks?

Emmy's information could have come from the day's headlines. Someone – or a group of someones – had been using the Miramar as a meeting place, somewhere to pass on faked identity cards and to collect the money when they sold. My guess was that Emmy had seen something she shouldn't have and was frightened enough to write it down. She hadn't actually mentioned any names, but her suspicions did make sense; with San Blanco being as close to the international border as it was, it made a perfect rendezvous for this type of business.

Ellie was silent, a small miracle as far as I was concerned, but I could see that she was mulling over the letter quite seriously. I was tempted to shout 'Boo!' as I used to do when we were younger, but that probably would have been a bad idea: Ellie loves to get revenge. Besides, our first gaggle of guests had arrived, and I needed to put on my Professional Concierge face.

Once the hubbub had died down and all had been given maps and directions to the area's attractions, Ellie and I sat back in our chairs in recovery mode. This was a bigger deal than I had suspected. I suppose it was because Emmy made it appear effortless. But another group was on its way and there were brochures to fold and more copies of area maps to be made. 'And time,' I said to Ellie, 'is a-wastin'.'

Leaving Ellie to guard the fort, I made my way to the back office area that housed hotel information such as room bookings and staff rosters, as well as an industrial-size copy machine and other typical office supplies. I quickly ran copies of the map that we handed out to guests, staring at the wall above without actually seeing anything. My mind was still trying to get a handle on the newest wrinkle at the Miramar, and I knew I needed to put in a call to the police department. That thought made my heartbeat pick up the pace. At least I had that to look forward to, I told myself with a smile. And maybe I'd get to hand Emmy's letter directly to Detective Baird.

I was deep in a world of my own, picturing Detective Baird cracking the case wide open because of the letter, and me the proud recipient of a commendation – and a kiss from the grateful detective – when the door behind me slowly opened. As I turned around to see who it was, the room was suddenly plunged into darkness. The door slammed shut and I could hear the sound of footsteps pounding down the corridor.

As I groped my way blindly across the office, feeling for the light switch, I had an awful thought: this was not an accident. Someone – maybe even the Miramar Murderer – had known I was in there. Why follow me? Was it to do with Emmy's letter? Anyway, if the message they'd tried to deliver was to keep my nose out, it had been received, very loud and very clear.

I all but fell into my chair behind the concierge's desk, the copies I'd just made sliding from my grasp and spilling across the floor. Ellie took one look at me and came around the desk to hug me, her hair a perfumed curtain over my face. I told her what had just happened, speaking through jaws that felt like they'd been wired shut. In a word, I was stunned. Not since Edmond had locked me in a closet, leaving me to scream and cry and pound on the door for five minutes before Aunt Amie had come to my rescue, had I felt like this. My stomach was in knots and the idea of even *touching* a cookie, much less eating one, made me feel like *losing* my cookies, in a manner of speaking.

I leaned into Ellie's embrace, willing my tense muscles and nerves to relax. Apparently Edmond's idea of a childhood joke had messed with my psyche a bit more than I'd realized.

'I think,' I began, looking up at Ellie, 'we need to call Detective Baird now. As in RIGHT NOW. I am not going to have something like that happen again, to me or to anyone else. Not to mention that next time it might be *sayonara* for yours truly.' I shuddered. That was definitely not on my job description.

'What I want to know is who had the bright idea to do that in the first place?' Ellie's question echoed my sentiments exactly. Who would even know that I had an inkling of what might be going on at the Miramar?

I opened the top desk drawer, fishing around until I found the card that Detective Baird had handed me that first night. I'd only kept it because I thought he was a cutie, and not because I intended to use it. That went to show how little *I* could predict the future.

I stopped short, my fingers frozen in mid-search. Predicting the future might just be the way to go with this one, and I just happened to have my own human crystal ball sitting right next to me. It couldn't hurt, and it might even help. Detective Baird, dimpled smile and all, would just have to wait a bit longer.

Chapter Thirteen

I sat back in my desk chair, eyeing my cousin. She must have had her radar going full force because she looked up at me, her own eyes narrowing in suspicion.

'Nope, AJ. Uh uh. No how, no way. I don't want to know anything else.' Ellie spoke adamantly, her hair flying around her shoulders as she shook her head.

'Aw, come on, cuz,' I cajoled, using the sweet voice that made my father melt and got me whatever I wanted (not that I'm proud of this or anything). 'You know you like messing with those cards. Tell me what you saw when you did that reading earlier. Or maybe do another little reading, just for me? Who knows? You might even solve this whole mess!'

Ellie loves flattery. Being known as the one who caught a killer would ice the cake for her. I could already visualize her trying to negotiate a TV show.

'Oh, all right,' she said, feigning disgust. 'But just this one time, AJ,' she added in a warning tone. 'This place gives me the creeps and I'm not too sure if I even want to know what's going on here or not.'

I hugged her. Ellie was nothing if not predictable. Before she could change her mind, I gave her a push, trundling her off to the suite in the hope that a quiet setting would help her concentrate. Not that I was a believer or anything, but if she was truly able read the future in the cards, I didn't want her to be distracted one iota.

The second bunch of guests kept me hopping for a

good half hour. I practically had to give a speech about the local attractions, which was funny, considering how new I was to the area. I know how to fake it, though, and managed to project a confidence I wasn't really feeling. My mind had slipped its tether and scampered down the hall towards my room. I was antsy, waiting for Ellie to reappear, and I was happy to see the last of the guests exit the front door.

When an hour had come and gone, and there was still no sign of Ellie, I began to get edgy. With everything that had already happened, including my little adventure in the dark, I couldn't shake the notion that something – or someone – was keeping her from returning.

I stood looking out at the sweeping views beyond the resort, uneasily chewing a thumbnail and debating whether or not to go and look for Ellie. Common sense told me I could just call her cell, but still I hesitated. My imagination had kicked into overdrive and created all sorts of scenarios. What if she were hiding in the closet or under the bed and her ring tone gave her away? I couldn't take the chance. I'd just have to go there myself and see what was what.

I have no idea what possessed me to go to my suite alone, but I did. Call it stupidity or blissful ignorance: I suppose I wanted to prove that nothing was amiss, that Ellie would be seated at my little kitchen table, concentrating on getting the cards' message.

The door was closed – no big surprise there. Ellie is always cautious about security when she goes to any big city. I jiggled the doorknob, but the automatic locking mechanism held firm. I had just lifted my hand to knock when I stopped short: I had to listen closely, but I could definitely hear the unmistakable sound of someone quietly moaning.

If you've ever found yourself in a 'situation', as my mother would say, complete with pounding heart and sweaty palms, then you'll know exactly how I was feeling at that moment. Unfortunately, I am one of those folks who tend to freeze when confronted with any type of emergency, and I couldn't get my mind to conjugate a single thought (at least not one that made any sense). I was like an ice sculpture, frozen in place and unable to move.

'Miss? Are you OK?' I turned my head to see the young girl who had brought our room service to us standing at the end of the corridor, a look of concern on her face.

'Call Security,' I managed to croak, backing away from the door. I grabbed for the wall just as my knees buckled.

It felt like an hour but I'm sure it was only minutes before I could hear the thump of running feet heading in my direction. In short order, three security guards had opened my door and had stepped inside, cautiously surveying the room. I felt a momentary sense of dread; what if Ellie wasn't even in there, that I'd imagined it all and panicked for nothing?

When I saw what had happened to Ellie, I wished with all my heart that it had been a false alarm.

The Miramar doesn't have a medical facility, *per se*, but we do have a first-aid station down near the entrance to the beach. It sees mostly sunburns, heat exhaustion, dehydration; things that didn't require an immediate emergency room visit. I was fairly certain, though, that they had never treated injuries like those Ellie had: eyes completely swollen shut from repeated blows to her face, marks on her throat that were rapidly becoming bruises, and cuts at the edge of her mouth where the gag had been pulled mercilessly taut. She looked like a casualty of war or the victim of a car accident, and I was unable to catch my tears in time when they finally let me see her.

'Oh, my God! Ellie, I am so, so sorry.' I pressed my

cheek to her head, careful to keep my touch light, even though I wanted to wrap my arms around her and hug her as tightly as I could.

''s OK,' she managed to mumble, not able to open her mouth very wide. To my amazement, she tried to smile.

Talk about strong – my cousin was one tough cookie. I almost felt sorry for the person who had done this to her; he – or she – had better watch their backs. Ellie Saddler was on their trail.

'We've got to stop meeting like this,' said a familiar voice behind me.

I straightened up and turned to look into eyes the color of the Pacific Ocean on a sunny day: bright, clear, and blue. For once, though, I didn't fall under his spell. In fact, something akin to fury, to rage, began to stir in my mind, and the tears of sorrow threatened to become tears of anger. Where had he been when we needed him?

'Detective. How nice to see you.' It would be difficult to miss the sarcastic undertone of my words, but he seemed oblivious. Maybe they taught all police officers how to grow thick skins in the academy. Either that, or else he had deliberately chosen not to get my drift.

'I need just a minute or two with her then you can come back in, OK?' His kind words almost undid my resolve to be angry. Before I could experience a total collapse, though, I bolted from the room. I needed to preserve what dignity I still had.

I could hear the wail of sirens as paramedics pulled in at the Miramar's front entrance. Even though the first-aid station wasn't within eyeshot of the resort, I imagined I could see the guests, faces glued to the windows, watching with unabated curiosity. It made me so mad that I almost hoofed it back to the resort to give them all a piece of my mind. I thought better of it, though, since any piece of my mind probably wouldn't be worth the time or effort. I was still reeling from the viciousness of Ellie's attack and I found that I was having trouble keeping my thoughts harnessed.

'She'll be OK, so don't worry, AJ.' Detective Baird had managed to walk up behind me without a sound, and naturally I jumped sky high.

'And she gave me a pretty good description of who it was." He gave a short laugh. 'She's pretty spunky. Told me she managed to scare them off by waving Tarot cards at them.'

Oh sure, I thought cynically. We've got some superstitious burglars on the loose. Aloud, I said, 'You make it sound like she tripped while walking on the beach,' I took a deep breath, trying to calm my heart that had thrown itself in panic against my ribs. 'Ellie, in case you hadn't noticed, was attacked by someone who wasn't out to make friends, not someone looking for a card reading.'

'I know,' he replied quietly. He stretched out a hand to touch my shoulder, then seemed to think better of it. I was in full-blown prickle mode and it showed.

Mercifully, the paramedics' arrival saved me from making a complete dope of myself. I had enough to worry about without adding 'village idiot' to my résumé, especially in front of Detective Baird.

He gave me one last look then turned to lead them into the first-aid station. I hesitated, wanting to be with Ellie but not wanting to see her in pain. I was a chicken and I knew it, but I also know my limits. If I passed out now, I'd be no good to either one of us, and I was honor-bound and determined to make someone pay.

Ellie's departure for the local emergency room left me feeling bereft and awkward, as though I was the new kid on the block and didn't know quite what to do with my time. Of course, I knew that I probably should have gone straight back to the concierge's desk, but found I had no desire to be within ten feet of the place. As far as I was concerned, Stan West could do the job himself. I was fed up. I made up my mind on the spot: as soon as Ellie could travel, we were out of here.

Chapter Fourteen

Thankfully, Ellie was discharged from the hospital within a few hours. Nothing was broken – certainly not her spunky attitude – and with a few days of rest, the attending doctor assured us, all the cuts and bruises would heal. Of course, Detective Baird had gone with her in the ambulance, playing the kindness card, but I was still upset. I know blaming him for the attack was pure nonsense, but he was an easy target.

True to my word, I gave my notice to Stan West, whose face went from resort tan to blanched pale in a matter of seconds. I knew him well enough by now to recognize the symptoms for what they were: he was far more concerned about having to cover the concierge station than he was for his employees' wellbeing. Whatever. If he pushed me enough, he'd find out exactly what he could do with his precious resort.

I was in the middle of packing my belongings, Ellie snoozing on the couch, when someone knocked on the door. The sound instantly awakened her and sent my heart thumping nearly out of my chest, but I managed to rearrange my face from 'scared to death' to 'it's only the door' so that Ellie wouldn't be further traumatized. I was feeling mighty responsible for her, despite the fact that she'd come here on her own accord.

'Who is it?' I queried, my words conveying my best no-nonsense, do-not-mess-with-me manner.

'It's me, miss.' I heard the soft voice of the young girl who'd called Security for me. 'I was just checking on you, to see how you are.'

I hesitated, still a bit wary. Did I dare open the door? Oh, what the heck. She'd practically been the hero of the moment, and I still needed to thank her for noticing my distress and getting hold of Security as quickly as she had. I flipped the deadbolt lock and unhooked the safety chain, stepping back to allow her entrance into the suite. With a timid smile, she came in.

Ellie, propped up on cushions to ease the pain in her neck and back, struggled to rise to a sitting position, but I quickly and gently pushed her back down. All I needed was another trip to the ER and an extra day or two here in San Blanco. The place was rapidly losing its charm, and even my family's reunion sounded tame compared to the chaos I'd experienced in just a few short days. That thought alone should have been evidence of my frame of mind. I was a nervous wreck and wanted out of here as fast as I could pack and hit the freeway.

The girl stood near the door, eyes looking uncertainly from me to Ellie and back to me again. I managed a smile, and stuck out my hand.

'I'm AJ, and I wanted to let you know how grateful I am for your help today.'

Her hand was as small and fragile as a child's, and I could see my words had embarrassed her. Still, she had a kind of dignity that made her seem surprisingly older than her years.

'I was happy to help, miss. I only wished that I could have done more for you. And her.' She looked over at Ellie again, and I read the concern in her eyes. Concern – and something else. And I had a feeling that this 'something else' was the real reason behind her visit.

My hackles were rising, and a swift glance at Ellie told me that we were on the same wavelength. If this girl – a look at her name badge told me her name was Dulce – knew something, or had heard anything, we needed to know. I still had Emmy's letter tucked away safely, but there had to be more to this whole mess than a bunch of men making fake identity cards.

'Please, sit down and visit for a few minutes. If you can, that is,' I added, noting the quick look Dulce gave to her wristwatch. The last thing I needed was to get her in hot water with the boss. He was plenty mad at me as it was.

'Yes, I can. I am on my break,' she answered. She settled herself on the edge of one of the armchairs, smiling shyly at me.

Ellie had somehow managed to raise herself up on her elbows. She gave a little groan and I all but flew to her side. That girl could be so stubborn, and it reminded me of the time we were riding our bikes and daring each other to jump across the tiny creek that ran behind my house. I had given up almost right away, not wanting to risk a fall or my mother's wrath for ruining my school clothes.

Not Ellie. It took her at least five tries, not to mention getting her clothes soaking wet and a few fresh cuts on her knees, before she mastered the jump. She was not about to give in, and that was how she approached life. This mishap was not going to keep her down. In fact, I'd be willing to bet that it fueled her desire to tackle the problem, to figure this whole thing out. I almost groaned along with her: call me intuitive, but I had a gut feeling that we were going to be here for longer than a day or two, if Ellie had anything to do with it.

One look at Dulce's face told me that she clearly had something on her mind. A sideways glance at Ellie confirmed she'd not only seen the look and recognized it for what it was, but also had her own motives for talking with the young girl. Knowing my cousin as well as I did, I assumed the conversation would end with a peek at the cards.

'I have heard, miss,' Dulce said, looking at Ellie, 'that

you can tell what will happen in the future.' She stopped, her eyes dropping to the floor as though the rest of her words were written there on invisible cue cards.

Ellie, bless her heart, gave Dulce the time she needed to compose her thoughts. I would have been tempted to jump in and coax the words out, but the silence seemed to work. Dulce raised her head and looked at Ellie with determination. She had made up her mind, it seemed, and was ready to talk.

'I am afraid, miss. Some of us here at the Miramar, we don't have papers, so we get the necessary things from some men who help us get jobs.' Dulce paused, waiting to see if we were comprehending what she was saying. I nodded at her encouragingly, having only a vague understanding of what she meant. Ellie, on the other hand, was staring back at Dulce. Either she knew exactly what the girl meant or she had zoned out on her pain medication.

Giving a little shake of her head, Dulce continued. 'This man they found, the one when the little girl was missing? He was one of the men who helped me and José get our papers. I think that someone wanted his business so they killed him.'

That pronouncement certainly got my attention. From a quick glance at Ellie, I could see she was following Dulce word for word. Thank goodness. I was afraid I'd have to confiscate her meds.

'Did that have anything to do with Miguel?' I asked the question without even thinking, but to my surprise, Dulce nodded soberly at me, her eyes troubled and sad.

'Yes, miss. Miguel, he used to work here. And I think that maybe he found out who was selling the papers.'

OK. I wasn't too sure where this was going, considering that Miguel obviously hadn't tattled to the authorities. I mean, Dulce was still here, wasn't she? If someone knew about the illegal papers and all that, wouldn't there have been a raid or whatever it was they did? I was a bit confused about the direction this conversation was taking.

Judging by the sudden light in Ellie's eyes, she'd made a connection that my brain hadn't. Swinging her legs very slowly over the edge of the sofa, she began to sit up. In a flash, Dulce had reached Ellie's side, gently slipping an arm under her shoulders and guiding her upright.

'Thanks, Dulce,' Ellie managed to get out. My crazy cousin apparently thought she could walk as well, because she tried to stand up, instead dropping heavily back onto the couch.

'OK, Iron Woman. You just stay right there,' I ordered, getting to my feet and walking over to where Ellie sat hunched over. 'If you need something, tell me. I can get it for you.' I was not about to let her hurt herself any further, even if it meant physically restraining her.

'I just need my cards,' Ellie retorted with a little of the old fire in her voice.

A good sign, I thought approvingly. Judging by the glare she gave me, she had read that thought. I stuck out my tongue and walked to the kitchen table to retrieve her precious cards.

Slowly, methodically, Ellie shuffled the deck of oversized cards and held them, looking over at Dulce. 'Tell me about the man who got the papers for you and your brother,' she said.

'He was a friend of my father's and lived not too far from us. When I was little, too small to remember, he came here and found work. It was much easier then,' added Dulce in a wistful voice.

Ellie laid out a row of cards on the coffee table. She nodded to Dulce. 'Go on. Tell me about working here at the Miramar. Did you know Miguel very well?'

I'd seen Ellie do her card thing before. I am not a believer in getting messages from inanimate objects, but

Ellie can make people think that whatever she tells them is exactly what they wanted – and needed – to hear, just by asking a few questions. I was curious how she'd handle the information Dulce was feeding her.

Dulce's face lit up. 'Oh, I love it here! It's not too far from my parents and I can see them whenever I can get some time off. And there are lots of nice-looking men, too,' she added shyly, her thin cheeks coloring with a becoming blush.

What is it with women who can make a blush look easy *and* elegant?

A small smile played around Ellie's mouth. Another good sign, I thought. She still had her sense of humor intact.

'And Miguel? How well did you know him?' Ellie prompted, continuing to lay the cards on top of one another in different patterns which looked completely random to me.

Dulce gave a little grimace. 'He was nice, and was a brother to my friend Maria, but …' She stopped, hesitating with her words.

'But what, Dulce?' I asked, a trifle impatiently. Between Ellie's pseudo-science and Dulce's reticence, this conversation was moving at a snail's pace.

Ellie shot me a look that told me, in very clear terms, to back off. This was *her* show, the look said, and she was going to run it the way she saw fit. I managed to keep myself from giving her one of my screwy faces from our childhood squabbles, the kind where I crossed my eyes and let my tongue hang out of my mouth. Poor Dulce was probably already spooked enough without me adding to it.

'His wife, she knew about Miguel and Emmy.' Dulce looked embarrassed to be repeating stories like this, but this was the good stuff, in my book.

Ellie flipped over a card, looked at it intently for a moment, then set it aside. I saw the minute shake of her head, and a tiny shiver tripped down my spine. Whatever she had seen on that card had made her uneasy. Looking up from the cards, Ellie nodded at Dulce, waiting for her to continue.

'When Miguel was hurt the other night – when he died – we all thought that maybe his wife had done something. Not to kill him,' she hastily added, 'Just to make him hurt enough to leave the Miramar and come home to her.'

Well, I suppose that did make sense, in a twisted way. Of course, a suspicious wife might have followed him and been here when the sound system was set up, but surely she would have been noticed by someone. I mean, even Emmy ... I let that thought go as another one filled my mind. Could it have been that *Emmy* was the target? I looked over at Ellie, my excitement building. Maybe I had stumbled onto part of the mystery.

'What, AJ?' Ellie sounded cross, as though I'd jumped up on stage in the middle of performance and grabbed the mike from her hand.

'Look,' I said, glancing from Ellie to Dulce. 'Let's say that Miguel's wife didn't want him back here, especially since he and Emmy ... well, since he and Emmy were close.' I checked to make sure that they were following me. 'Maybe his wife knew Emmy would be the one to make sure everything was in working order, you know, the sound system was OK and the instruments in place. Could she have rigged it up so that Emmy would have been the one to get the shock, only it misfired a bit and Miguel was the one who got it instead?' I stopped, out of words and out of breath.

Ellie just stared at me, eyes narrowing a bit as the wheels turned. Dulce, on the other hand, had opened her eyes as wide as they would go, looking like a little deer in the headlights of a fast-moving big rig.

'So how would you explain Emmy?' demanded Ellie. She, poor thing, was still traumatized at the sight on the beach and needed a better story than a vengeful wife.

'This way,' I said eagerly, plopping down on the floor beside the couch. 'Miguel's death was an accident, so she needed to finish up the job because she knew that, eventually, Emmy would guess what had happened and would spill the beans.'

Ellie's look was one of disgust. She was not finding my train of thought easy to board, it seemed.

'And what about the letter? And the first dead man? And the illegal identity business or ring or conspiracy or whatever you call it? How do you make sense of all that?'

I waited for – and got – the famous Ellie hair toss; the one that said that I was a goofball and had no idea what I was saying. One quick peek at Dulce told me that she agreed with Ellie, although she softened her judgment with a little smile.

Well, if I didn't know what I was talking about, I knew someone who did. And I sure could use a dimple just about now. Fishing Detective Baird's card from my pocket, I got to my feet and headed for the phone. It was time to call in the big guns, no pun intended.

Chapter Fifteen

'What are you doing?' exclaimed Ellie, one hand arrested in mid-flip of another card. 'We've almost got this whole thing figured out, AJ!'

What she *really* meant was that she was almost done with her card trick – which is how I thought of it – and the police could just wait a dang minute until she'd solved the crime for them. I almost rolled my eyes but thought better of it in the nick of time; I needed Ellie as an ally, not an enemy.

'Well, hurry it up then, O Great Seer.' This earned me a glare, which I blithely ignored. Ellie took herself way too seriously sometimes. 'We still need to tell the detectives about the letter. I don't know about you, but I have no desire to be arrested or put in thumbscrews or whatever it is they do when you withhold vital evidence.'

'Whatever,' Ellie muttered, bending back over the table and passing a hand over the cards.

I ignored that quip as well. I figured the faster she got done, the faster I could make that call. I was beginning to feel twitchy for some reason, but Ellie wasn't on the same wavelength. I was probably being paranoid, but I couldn't shake the idea that the answer was closer than we thought.

A sharp rap on the door made us all jump sky high. Dulce was on her feet in one second flat, a hand pressed to her heart and the other held to her mouth. Her eyes stared at me over her hand, and she looked scared. Actually, she looked petrified, and I didn't think it had anything to do with taking too long on her break. Dulce was frightened of whoever stood on the other side.

Edging quietly to the door, I waited a moment before I called out, 'Who is it?'

I thought I could hear a slight shuffling noise, but I couldn't identify it. No name, no open door, I thought grimly. I wasn't about to invite the killer into my suite.

'Ms Burnette? It's Detective Fischer. I just need to speak with you for a moment and your cousin, if she's still here.' The officer's gruff voice came through the door, and my heart completed a gymnastic flip that would have been scored a ten as it settled back inside my chest. Not quite the detective I had in mind, but he'd do.

I undid the safety chain and unlocked the door. Detective Fischer was standing in the corridor, a battered notebook in one hand. He was flipping through the pages, stopping every now and then to read what was there. I only hoped it didn't say anything about a certain letter. I was sure that 'guilty' was written all over my face.

'Come in, Detective,' I invited, standing aside to allow him entrance into the suite.

Dulce had retreated to one of the armchairs, hands clasped together and feet pulled back under the chair as though she was trying to hide them. Ellie merely glanced up briefly, nodding while keeping her focus on the three cards she now had laying face up.

Without a word, Detective Fischer walked over to the table, hands behind his back, head moving back and forth as he gazed at the colorful display. I held my breath, waiting for him to do the forbidden and reach out to take a card. To my relief, he did not, seemingly content to wait until Ellie was ready to speak. Maybe he wasn't as dense as I'd thought. Of course, I suspected I was a tad preferential of a certain someone's smile, but hey! I could focus when I needed to.

'What can we do for you, Detective?' Ellie looked up calmly, hands held loosely in her lap and the three cards left ignored on the table. She'd share when she was ready.

'I have a few more questions for the two of you,' Detective Fischer replied, his gaze sweeping the rest of the room and settling on Dulce. 'If I could have a minute?'

Dulce got his semi-subtle hint, leaping to her feet and scuttling toward the door. 'I will see you in a few days, if that is OK? It is my scheduled time off work but I would love to visit with you again.' With a shy smile, she was out the door and gone.

I settled onto the couch next to Ellie, tucking my feet up and relaxing back against the cushions. I was certain this would take more than a mere minute and I wanted to be comfortable while I tried to decide whether or not to confess to the letter from Emmy.

My cousin, I noticed, had also settled back against the pillows, moving slowly to give her sore body time to adjust. The fact that she was moving at all was a great improvement, though, and I mentally moved our escape from the Miramar from two days to one. We could just make the drive back up the coast a bit more leisurely than the trip down.

'Do you mind?' Detective Fischer indicated the chair that Dulce had just vacated, settling his bulk into it before either one of us could reply. Not that we'd ever tell an officer 'No', but really! "The manners of some folks," as my mother would point out with a dainty sniff.

Neither Ellie nor I spoke, putting the onus of the interview back on the detective's shoulders. I'd read somewhere that silence, like Nature, abhors a vacuum, and was waiting to see what Detective Fischer would fill it with. Finally, with a dramatic sigh that indicated being very put upon by two recalcitrant women, he spoke.

'I understand,' he said, looking straight at me, 'that you might have something I need to take a look at.'

I was startled, no doubt about it. Was he psychic as well? Or had I just looked so guilty when I opened the door that he could read my face, no need for cards. My mouth opened and shut a few times as though on a trial run as I tried to gather my scattered wits back into one area.

'Well,' I said, stammering slightly. 'I have, er ... a letter that, er ... may have something to do with this.' My right hand indicated Ellie, who now sat looking like a martyr of the purest ilk. My cousin, I may have mentioned before, loves not only the limelight, she also knows how to play to an audience. Hence the slightly drooping eyes, the listless hands, the down-turned mouth. I couldn't look at her for fear I'd burst into hysterical laughter, thus ensuring that we'd both be hauled off to the nearest loony-bin, if not the San Blanco jail.

Detective Fischer, to his credit, did not say a word. He merely held out a hand in silent appeal, and I acquiesced, uncurling my legs and walking over to the kitchen. I had hidden the missive in the freezer beneath a bag of ice, and the envelope felt a bit stiff. I was sure it was still readable, though. Thankfully, whoever had been in my suite had not thought to look there; I was still certain that the entire chaotic mess hinged on Emmy's last words to me.

Brushing off a few pieces of ice that had clung to the paper, Detective Fischer carefully opened the envelope and tipped the letter out onto his lap. He peered into the envelope before laying it aside and taking up the piece of paper, reading it through at least twice before making eye contact with me again.

'When did you get this?' he asked, flapping the limp letter at me. 'And from where, if I might ask?' Of course he could ask. He was the police, after all.

I stared back at him, my mind a sudden blank. Where had I gotten it? And when?

My days and nights at the Miramar all seemed to run together in my mind, so much had happened in less than a week. I looked at Ellie for help, hoping she'd have better recall than I did at that moment.

'Maria,' she prompted me, reaching a soft hand over to mine and giving it a squeeze. 'And Fernando. Remember?'

And then I did, seeing clearly in my mind's eye the look on Maria's face when she handed me the letter, confessing to finding it in Emmy's room. I hesitated, wondering how much I needed to share. I had made Maria a promise, after all, albeit tempered with a mental finger-crossing. I honestly didn't want to get her in trouble; she had been honest enough to bring me the letter and frightened enough to beg anonymity. Still …

I took a deep breath, more to steady my thoughts than my nerves. Looking Detective Fischer square in his dull blue eyes (dull in comparison to you-know-who's pair of sparklers), I told him the entire tale, leaving nothing out, not even Maria's clandestine visit to Emmy's room. He listened attentively, stopping me occasionally to write something in his notepad, but otherwise focusing intently on my words. I began with my first horrific day on the job and ended with my experience in the darkened office.

When I'd finished, Detective Fischer just sat quietly, as though trying to take in what I'd told him. I admit, it did sound a bit fantastic but, considering everything that had happened to me and to Ellie, I hoped he'd take the situation seriously. I certainly did, and I know that Ellie did as well – and she had the bumps and bruises to prove it.

Shuffling his feet, Detective Fischer stood up. He gave me and Ellie a grim look, then said, 'If I were you, I'd keep my door locked at all times, even if you're just, say, running out for cookies.' This was directed at me, and I blushed. Even the San Blanco PD knew about my addiction to sugar, apparently. Was nothing around here sacred?

'I'll be in touch. If you don't mind, I need to keep this a while.' Waggling the letter in the direction of the couch, he reached the door and opened it. 'Lock this behind me.'

With that, he was gone.

I obediently walked over and flipped the security latch and then hooked the safety chain back. Ellie was quiet for a change, and I was trying to understand what had just happened. The SBPD was on to some leads, that was clear, and Detective Fischer had listened to my tale without recrimination or comment. That pointed to progress, in my book. Maybe Ellie and I were on the right trail, after all.

A gentle rumbling in my tummy reminded me that it had been a while since I'd eaten anything substantial, other than the odd cookie. I smiled, recalling the detective's 'cookie' comment, then paused mid-thought. What he'd said, in no uncertain terms, was that the killer – the Miramar Murderer – was roaming the corridors of the resort. Not quite the amenity I'd had in mind when I'd taken the job, that was certain. And probably not what Miguel, Emmy, and the mystery man had anticipated, either.

I needed to eat. I could not think on an empty stomach, and had no desire to join the rest of the curious faces in the Palmetto Room for dinner. I looked at Ellie. She lay back against the sofa, eyes closed and purple smudges under them adding up to a look of utter exhaustion. It would be room service, I decided, reaching for the phone to place an order. Of course, that meant someone else would have to walk the corridors of the resort, but hopefully they'd get our food to us before the killer discovered anyone out and about.

The omelets and fresh fruit, delivered by a young man with a solemn face, were delicious. The spinach and mushroom filling, along with a combination of Swiss and sharp cheddar cheeses, made mine one of the best omelets I'd ever had. Ellie had cleaned her plate as well, I noted, happy that she had enough energy to eat at least. Coming from a family that believed in the sanctity of mealtimes, I was always pleased to see others enjoying their food. And, as long as we had room service, we could hide out in the Palo Verde suite until we left this place.

Chapter Sixteen

I guess my Big Plan was to hole up in the suite like two criminals on the lam, live off of food delivered to our door, and sneak out in the dead of night – or whenever the San Blanco PD said we could go. I was voting for soon, although another *tête-à-tête* with Detective Cutie Pie might make me hang around a bit longer.

Leaving the tray out in the hall, I plumped myself back onto the couch. Ellie hadn't moved except for a quick trip to the bathroom, and I was too wound up to relax much. What I really wanted to do, I thought with surprise, was to get out and see what was up. Maybe I'd spot someone walking around with a conventioneer's name badge that would read, 'Hello! My Name is the Miramar Killer!' Huh. If only it were that easy. Of course, there'd be no need for detectives having to detect, and that would eliminate the chances of seeing a certain someone any time soon. Sigh. Such is life.

I thoroughly intended for us to hit the hay at a decent hour. Ellie needed her rest and I did as well; the day's events had tired me out more than I'd realized, although that was nothing compared to Ellie's harrowing day. Still, the two of us were in the deficit column for sleep and needed to rectify that soon.

We'd just made up our minds to begin our nightly rituals when the phone rang. Toothbrush in hand, I went to answer it, blithely singing out a greeting. I was met with silence, so once again I spoke.

'This is AJ,' I said, waving my toothbrush in the air

like a wand.

'You need to leave the Miramar. *Now*.' The voice was low, muffled, as if whoever it was had placed their hand over the mouthpiece in an attempt at camouflage, and they made no attempt to sound pleasant.

The dial tone after the pronouncement buzzed loudly in my ear as I stood, phone still in hand. If I didn't have the creeps before, they were firmly in place now, skipping up and down my spine as though they owned the place. They wanted me to leave *now?* I wanted to leave yesterday. I'd had it with this place.

Ellie appeared in the doorway to the bedroom, cold cream on her face and a look of concern in her eyes.

'AJ? What's up?' She walked into the front room, her steps a little slower than her normally spritely gait.

I still held the phone and looked at it as though it could give Ellie an answer. I had no words for her. I was heading from 'scared' towards 'angry' at a pretty fast clip, and it was all I could do not to throw it against the wall. A satisfying gesture, certainly, but I figured it wouldn't really be too smart to start destroying the place. With gritted teeth, I replaced it calmly.

'AJ?' she asked again. She was beginning to sound more than a little alarmed. 'Should I call someone?' She looked around the room as though she'd find a detective or two hanging out, ready to jump to our aid.

'Absolutely,' I said, then stopped. Who *would* we call? The Miramar's security team? I was fairly sure they were tired of all the AJ-centered drama already, although they'd probably do their job without comment. No, I didn't want to bother them again.

'Fernando,' I said without thinking. The name surprised me as well, popping out the way it did. Maybe, subconsciously, I knew he'd have an answer or two for us.

'OK,' agreed Ellie, a tad doubtfully. I guess her idea of 'someone' to call didn't include the resort's valet.

I moved to pick up the phone again, but the spread of cards on the table caught my eye. Ellie hadn't bothered to put them away, but left them where she had laid them. The three cards she had flipped over still lay on top of the rest, their message silent. Maybe, before we called anyone ...

'Ellie,' I said suddenly, 'what was it you were seeing before Detective Fischer stopped by? You never said.'

She stood looking at me, her eyes somber and the bruises on her neck and face more pronounced than ever. Even the cold cream couldn't cover them.

'Are you sure you want to know?' she asked, watching me carefully for my reaction.

I laughed, but it sounded forced. 'Of course, silly goose! I wouldn't have asked if I hadn't wanted to.' I made as if to pick up the three top cards but she moved quickly, more quickly than I thought she could, grabbing my wrist tightly.

'Don't, AJ.' Ellie sounded serious, and I looked at her in surprise. What in the world was wrong with touching a few pieces of cardboard with pictures on them?

I said nothing, moving back to let her retrieve the cards. She stood motionless, staring at them one after the other, her lips moving slightly. Finally, she looked up.

'Let me get this stuff off of my face first,' she said, slipping the cards into the pocket of her robe and walking back toward the bathroom.

I wandered into the kitchen, looking for something to snack on. I would *not* call for cookies and hot tea, although my body was screaming at me to just do it. Finding a few tea bags lying rejected in one of the drawers, I got out two mugs and filled them with water, intending to heat them up in the microwave.

What made me hesitate was a noise. Not the soft shuffling sound of paper, like there'd been with Detective Fischer, nor the sound of muted footsteps in the carpeted corridor. Something – someone – was gently turning the doorknob. I stood frozen, wanting to scramble for the bedroom and Ellie, to grab my cellphone and call the police. Instead, I watched in fascination as the doorknob seemed to come alive, turning one way and then the other, each twist louder and more determined than the one before. If someone wanted to get rid of me – to scare me off – they should have just told me. With all the weird vibes at the Miramar, I would have happily packed up and out the door in a heartbeat.

I shivered. The doors were not the sturdiest, in my opinion, and only a security lock and a wimpy safety chain – what a misnomer – were keeping them out. Making up my mind, I crept as quietly as I could over to the armchairs and picked one up, carrying it over so that it stood in front of the door. Thankfully, I had closed the drapes after we'd eaten, so at least no one could see in. The next step was to wedge the chair under the doorknob, but how I could do this without alerting them that I knew they were out there was beyond me.

Ellie, face fresh from being washed free of the cold cream, watched me with consternation. She hadn't heard the would-be intruder, so I probably looked like a nutcase to her. Making frantic signs with my hands, and mouthing the word 'killer' at her (dramatic, I know), I turned back to my present problem. I needed to get the door reinforced before I could call for help.

A loud crashing sound made me jump back and both of us scream. They had given up on the doorknob and were now throwing something – a shoulder, maybe – against the door, the sound echoing down the corridor. They couldn't possibly think that no one would hear them, could they?

I abruptly recalled seeing an announcement earlier inviting resort guests to 'Join us tonight on the beach for campfire, food, and fun!' Great. There was probably no one left in the entire hotel, and no one to hear the racket of someone trying to break down our door. I looked over at

Ellie, standing stock-still with a look of complete terror on her face. If we were going to make it through this, I needed her functioning, not comatose.

'Ellie!' I strode over to her, placing my hands on her shoulders and talking directly into her face. 'Look at me! It's OK! It'll be fine, I promise. Just help me get this chair wedged under the doorknob, then use your cell to call for help.'

She blinked once then gave herself a little shake as though awakening from a dream. Together we got the chair moved and turned on its side so that one chair leg fit snugly under the door knob. I was past caring if they heard us or not; in fact, I *wanted* them to know that we knew they were there and wouldn't go down without a fight. Or without a chair or two as a barricade.

Out of the blue, just as quickly as the din had started, it was gone. I hadn't heard whoever it was walking away from the door, but they must have. I felt brave enough to peek out through a corner of the drapery, hunkered down on my knees below the windowsill. No one was there. As far as I could see to the left or right, the corridor was empty. Ellie and I were safe. For now.

I grabbed for the phone, punching in 911 with shaking fingers. It seemed an eternity before I heard, '911, what's your emergency?'

'Someone just tried to break into our room at the Miramar Resort!' I know I sounded hysterical, but how would you expect me to sound? I tried to focus as the emergency operator took down the information and assured me that help was on the way. Did I want her to remain on the line until the police arrived?

'No, that's OK,' I answered, my fingers twisting through my hair the way I used to do when I was much younger and nervous about a test at school. Or whenever I needed to confess something to my parents, which was fairly often.

Ellie and I huddled on the couch together for support. My teeth were chattering, something that I thought only happened in the movies, and my knees had a funny, jelly-like feel. I hoped I'd be able to stand up and walk to the door when the police arrived.

'You know what, AJ?' Ellie's voice sounded much calmer than I was feeling. She always did have more stamina than I did. 'I don't think they were trying to break in.'

I had no answer for her – I couldn't make my mouth move. What in the world did she think had just happened? Of course someone was trying to break in!

'I just think they were trying to frighten us off. Remember the phone call?'

She did make sense, I had to admit. If they'd wanted to get in, a swift kick on the door to force open the safety chain would have done the trick.

The faint sound of rapidly moving feet heading in our direction made us both sit up. Crap! I'd completely forgotten about the chair. I'd need to get that moved before anyone could get in, even the police.

A knock on the door sent my heart into overdrive, but I managed to call out, 'Hang on! I need to take the chair away.' With a few tugs and pulls, I got the furniture shifted. Hopefully it was the San Blanco police on the other side.

Otherwise, I'd just made it plenty easy for the Miramar Murderer to join us for tea.

Chapter Seventeen

I think it took Ellie and me at least three tries to explain what had happened to us, beginning with the threatening phone call.

'Did you recognize the voice?' The young officer taking our statements sat at the kitchen table while we huddled together on the sofa.

'No, I didn't, and I told Detective Fischer that earlier when he was here.' Now that I'd semi-recovered from the shock, I was becoming irritated at having to repeat things I'd said only hours before. Didn't these people ever read one another's notes and reports?

The officer just nodded his blond crew-cut as he continued writing, and I slid Ellie a sideways glance that said *one more inane question and I'll implode* or something to that effect. I think she got the message.

Standing gingerly to her feet, Ellie approached the table. 'Officer Phillips?' She ducked her head to read his badge. 'My cousin and I have had a fairly difficult day.' That was the understatement of the year, I thought. 'Right now we could use something to drink so I need to call room service.' The officer must've have given her a certain look, because she hastily added, 'Just some hot tea, Officer. That's all.'

The officer nodded and turned to face me. 'I have just a few more questions then I'll get out of your hair, OK?'

Either the kitchen staff had absolutely nothing else to do or they'd already heard about our little escapade and wanted the scoop, because within five minutes of Ellie's call we had a plateful of hot cookies and a steaming pot of tea. When I opened the door to a gentle knock, I was glad to see Maria again, especially since I'd been a little worried over the letter issue. If the killer knew I had the letter, surely he (or she) would realize who had given it to me.

'Can you stay for a moment?' I asked Maria, hoping she'd be able to read between the lines. I was counting on the officer's promise that he'd be gone in a few minutes; then I could get down to business and talk to Maria about the letter.

Thankfully, she caught the meaning. 'Yes, I'd be happy to stay with you until you are done with your tea.' She walked over to where Ellie stood in the small kitchen and gently pushed her toward the couch. 'You go and sit, Miss Ellie. I can take care of this.'

True to his word, Officer Phillips left after a few more questions ('Did you get a look at their face?' and so on) and exited the suite with a solemn reminder for us to relock the door behind him. I almost snorted. Did he really think that *not* locking it was an option for me?

After making sure the door was totally secure and an armchair moved in front of it 'just in case ...' (I didn't finish the thought, not wanting to consider what the 'in case' might consist of), I sank to the floor near the coffee table and laid my head on my arms. I was tired to the bone and so weary of all the drama.

Ellie sat on the couch with the forgotten cards in her hands, looking down at them as though she wasn't really seeing them at all. I wondered what she had seen earlier, when she'd turned them over and then clammed up. Maybe it was time for her to share.

'Ellie,' I began, lifting my head to look her in the eyes, 'I think it's about time for you to explain the cards to us.' I nodded at the cards, noting that one in particular she held on to tightly. 'Start with that one, OK?'

Ellie's eyes were composed, her face an almost blank surface. Aside from the marks and bruises from her attack, she looked calm. In a voice that betrayed no emotion, she said, 'I will tell you about only one card. The others ... well, they are after the fact. This card,' she held it toward me so that I could see the picture of a man who stood looking skyward, holding a flower in one hand and a bundle in the other, 'this is The Fool, the main player in the story. He is not as harmless as he looks, and can change to become whatever it is you want to see. He is very, very dangerous.'

Okaaaay, I thought. That was obviously the bad guy, the killer. But who did we know that could change himself to become something else altogether? It sounded like we should be looking for an overgrown chameleon.

'Do you mean he can be someone who is nice to one person and mean to someone else?' Maria timidly asked, her brow furrowed as she tried to understand Ellie's meaning.

'Yes and no,' Ellie replied, replacing the card on her lap, face down. 'It will be someone we think to be one way who is really another. He will be very good at disguising who he really is.'

Great. According to Ellie, now we were looking for someone who could be anybody, really, since most of us tend to be different people in different situations. And that, I thought, was proof positive why I'd never fall for the cards and their so-called 'messages from beyond'; they made absolutely no sense to me and just got folks riled up. Besides, we tend to believe what we want to, cards or no cards. I just shook my head.

We three sat there quietly, each of us isolated within our own thoughts. I was contemplating the trip home, already thinking about Ellie and whether or not she'd be able to drive herself back. I'd figured that a two-day trip would be OK, especially if we timed it so we stopped near the vineyard that offered public tasting. We could stay the night somewhere nearby.

The phone rang, startling us all back to the present. Ellie and I looked at each other, not wanting to answer it for fear of what we'd hear. Maria, sensing our hesitation, reached over and picked up the receiver.

'Hello? Ms Burnette's room,' she said, and then a broad smile lit up her face. 'Of course! I will wait until you get here. Yes, we are fine. That would be very nice. *Gracias*, Fernando.'

I let out the breath I hadn't even realized I'd been holding. It was only Fernando, the valet and – I suspected – Maria's 'special someone'. He was a person I could trust, I felt, especially since he'd shown such concern over Emmy's letter.

'That was Fernando,' Maria announced. 'He's on his way to get me, to walk me back to the kitchen. And he'll bring something for you "as a midnight snack", he said.'

'Oh, that wasn't necessary,' I protested, but not very vigorously. Snacks at any time of the day or night were fine by me. Living at the Miramar had definitely spoiled me in the cooking department, and I dreaded having to make my own meals again. On the other hand, if I stayed here much longer, I might not be alive to eat any more of the wonderful things that came out of the Miramar kitchen.

Fernando arrived, carrying a tray of goodies that almost boggled the mind. I'd expected a few small pastries, perhaps a bag or two of popcorn for the microwave and the ubiquitous cookies, but what he'd brought surpassed even my imagination: small croissants, some drizzled with chocolate and almonds and some filled with cream cheese; two glass bowls of sliced fruit and small containers of various dipping sauces; and something that looked like miniature burritos, rolled tightly and arranged on a plate around a bowl of guacamole. Good Lord, I thought, if we actually eat all this as a late-night snack, they'll have to roll the two of us out to our cars. But I was certainly willing to chance it.

'Thanks, Fernando.' I smiled at him. He looked embarrassed but pleased, and I could see the way Maria was looking at him. It was obvious that she had it bad.

After the couple left, holding hands and each smiling into the other's face, I curled up on the couch next to Ellie. We were both exhausted, but I wasn't sure if I'd be able to relax enough to fall asleep. We needed to, though, especially if we were driving back home tomorrow. I leaned my head back on the cushions and could feel myself starting to drift off. I must have fallen asleep almost instantly, because the next thing I knew, Ellie's hand was on my shoulder and her mouth was close to my ear.

'AJ!' she hissed. 'I swear I heard something out in the corridor. Get up and look!'

Me? Get up and look? I was still too groggy from my short nap to move from the couch. Next moment a sound, like breaking glass, sent the two of us flying across the room. I couldn't tell where it was coming from, and I sure as heck wasn't volunteering to open the door and find out. Instead, I clung to Ellie's arm, more awake now than I'd ever been before.

We stood, ears straining, listening for more sounds.

'It's as if it's right outside the door,' Ellie whispered. I had to agree.

Someone was cursing softly, and I could hear a tinkling, like glass being picked up. Taking a breath, I shook myself loose from Ellie's grip and inched over to the window, cautiously lifting up an edge of the drapery.

I almost laughed aloud in relief. A man in a kitchen staff uniform was kneeling on the carpet, an empty tray near him. A dark slick of something wet covered the carpet, ice cubes tossed around like so many diamonds. The sound we'd heard was just him dropping a full pitcher of iced tea.

I glanced over at Ellie. She looked awful and, I could tell, was all the worse for the lack of sleep. She so desperately needed rest. Come to think of it, so did I. I double-checked the locks on the door, flicked the curtain back into place, and yawned so loudly that I was sure the man in the hall could hear.

'Come on, Ellie. Let's get some sleep.' I walked toward the bedroom, my legs feeling as though they weighed a ton. Maybe things wouldn't be so bad tomorrow, I thought. Correction, I said to myself: *hopefully* things won't be as bad tomorrow. I wasn't sure if I could take anything else.

The light from beyond the bedroom window woke me next morning. I must have slept like the dead – not good phraseology, but apropos here at the Miramar – and Ellie looked as though she hadn't stirred either. We'd both fallen asleep in the king-size bed, our backs to one another like we used to do when we'd sleep over at each other's house. Long ago, we'd decided this was the best way to catch any monsters who dared creep in at night and get us, and that logic was never truer. Of course, we'd have to be awake to actually *see* an intruder, but still we'd both sleep well, conscious that we had each other's backs.

I lay there a few minutes more, trying to decide what to do about breakfast. That was a good omen, I decided. Being more concerned with what I was going to eat than worrying about a killer on the loose meant that I was far less stressed.

I think if I could have seen what the day held in store for me, I might have just stayed in bed. Too bad I didn't believe in foretelling the future.

Chapter Eighteen

I sat back on the couch, my feet on the coffee table and hands clasped over a full tummy. I was as close to miserable as I'd been in quite a while. I'd eaten so much my stomach actually hurt, but was it ever worth it! The kitchen crew had outdone itself this morning: golden brown omelets oozed melted cheese, encasing a mélange of red and green peppers, mushrooms, and onion (I'd had so many of these already at the Miramar, but why stop a good thing?); crispy bacon with just the right amount of succulent fat left on the slices (that is always my favorite part, I have to admit); fresh fruit and yogurt topped with the resort's homemade granola and toasted almonds; freshly squeezed orange juice; and a steaming carafe of coffee. I was in "hog heaven", as my dad likes to say after a good meal.

Unfortunately, evil had invaded *this* hog heaven, this paradise. The Miramar, its appeal lost in a miasma of malevolence, was no longer the dream place to work. As I sat with my eyes closed, resting and waiting for Ellie to get out of the shower, I thought about everything that had happened. If I hadn't experienced it for myself, I would not have believed it.

I heard the shower water stop, and I maneuvered my feet onto the floor, giving a slight groan. I figured that if I lived on bread and water for the next month or two, I could lose the poundage gained in the week I'd been in San Blanco. And knowing Ellie the way I did, I was sure she'd be back into her crazy exercise regime as soon as she could move without pain. She was my own built-in boot camp fitness instructor.

I walked into the bedroom, ready to begin packing my few belongings. If you believe in destiny, it had certainly been at work in my case. I'd only packed enough for a week's worth of clean clothes, and that was all I needed, as it turned out. I sighed, remembering Emmy's elegant style of dress and her delightful laugh, her sweet way of handling even the most difficult guest. What an absolute waste. She'd been one of the few genuine folks I'd ever met, a real what-you-see-is-what-you-get woman, and it was particularly rare, because she was my boss. I'd be lucky to work for someone like her again.

I opened the closet. My new suitcase, bought especially for this little adventure, sat in lonely splendor on the top shelf. As I reached up to grab it and gave it a tug, something white fluttered to the ground. I just stared at it for a moment, trying to figure out where it came from. Presumably it had been on the shelf before I'd placed the suitcase there, and the dragging motion had dislodged it.

I stooped down and picked up the paper from the closet floor. Turning it over, I saw it was Miramar stationery, available in every suite and in the main lobby. I could see nothing written on it though, so I tossed it on the bed. Maybe I'd keep it for a souvenir, or 'silver ear', as Ellie and I liked to say. (We also said 'itch-a-ma-skitch' in place of 'mosquito', so go figure.)

The bathroom door opened, emitting an invigorating scent of lemon grass and mint. Ellie loved her bath products, and she always managed to find a combination that I never would have considered. On her, though, they always smelled awesome. I turned to smile at her, noting that she was moving a bit more easily.

'It's all yours,' Ellie said, rubbing her hair with one of the Miramar's luxurious towels. 'If you want, you can use some of my body wash.'

'I hope you left some hot water,' I grumbled playfully, giving Ellie's shoulder a gentle pat as I walked by toward the still steamy bathroom. When we were younger and would spend the night with Grandma Saddler, it was always a fight to see who'd get to take a bath first. The second little girl would be in for a quick cold dip, thanks to the old-fashioned water heater that held just enough for one tub of water.

I chose a bath over a shower; somehow, it always evoked a sense of calm for me in the way a shower couldn't, no matter how many body washes claimed to be 'relaxing'. The Miramar sure knew how to pamper its guests, I thought dreamily, splashing my toes in the frothy foam that covered the water like fresh snow. As much as I enjoyed my stay, though, I realized I was still just a small-town girl who enjoyed the simpler things in life. Of course, I was pretty sure my view on the Miramar was tainted by the murder and mayhem I'd experienced first-hand. There's nothing like finding a dead body or two to put you off a good time.

Finally the water became tepid and the bubbles all but vanished. Reluctantly, I got myself out and dried part-way, throwing my robe over damp skin. Ellie thinks I'm weird, but I've never been one for drying off completely. Since she's never done it herself, I don't know how she can dismiss it. I say, don't knock it 'til you've tried it.

Ellie was still in her robe, damp hair trailing over one shoulder. She was sitting on the edge of the bed nearest the window, holding the piece of Miramar stationery up to the light as though trying to decipher a secret code.

'What's up with the paper, Ellie?' I ran a comb through my wet hair, being careful to start at the ends and work my way up, just like my mother had taught me. Actually, I tend to do most of the things she worked so hard to teach me, although to hear her tell it, I'm a lost cause.

'I can almost see something ...' she said, her eyes

examining the paper closely. 'It's like when you write something, the paper underneath can show what was written. You know,' she added, turning to look at me. 'Like those old detective shows, where someone finds a clue in an empty notebook.'

Huh? How could someone find a clue in an empty notebook? It would seem to me that empty meant just that – nothing there. My face must have betrayed me, because Ellie made the little disgusted noise she does whenever someone irks her. Like I was doing now, apparently.

'Not *empty* empty, ding dong.' Ellie thrust the paper at me. 'Here, take it. Hold it up to the window and tell me what you see.' She stood and took the towel from her head, tossing it into the bathroom. Thank goodness housekeeping was scheduled for today. It was beginning to look like my college dorm room in here.

I obediently held the paper up close to the window. There were a few faint markings, but nothing I could decipher. I had no idea what Ellie thought she was seeing. For all I knew, it might have been a list of places that the last guest wanted to visit. It wasn't anything to write home about.

Ellie was back, looking over my shoulder, staring hard at the stationery. Abruptly she pointed to one spot near the bottom.

'Look, AJ! You can just make out a name. Can you see it?' She sounded excited, intense, like she always does whenever something gets her attention.

I squinted, did the whole trombone arm thing folks do when they need bifocals and won't admit it. There was something there, a very faint outline that might have said 'Jos' or maybe 'Jas'. I couldn't really tell if there were any other letters, and these made no sense to me at all.

'I'm not seeing what you're seeing, Ellie,' I admitted, handing the paper back. I didn't need to worry; she'd make sure that I knew what it said. She was predictable that way.

'Look. Right here. It's a 'J', an 'O', and an 'S'. And I think this could be an 'A'. Or maybe it's an 'E'.' Ellie did everything except take my chin in her hand and guide my eyes across the paper. Maybe I did see those letters, but it could have just been suggestion. If she said that's what she saw, though, who was I to argue?

'What do you think it is? A letter? A list?' I walked over to the bathroom and dropped my towel on the floor next to Ellie's. When I got back home, I'd have to learn all over again how to take care of myself. It's amazing how you can get used to having someone else take care of all the day-to-day things, like cleaning and cooking.

Plus, at the Miramar, someone was taking care of killing.

Ellie stared at me as if I'd just grown a horn in the middle of my forehead, and I almost reached up to see if something was there. Ellie has that effect on me at times.

She held the paper up to the light again, this time moving her finger carefully across the paper.

'I see it! Absolutely! Yes! AJ, you are a marvel!' She whirled around and threw her arms around me, then yelped. 'Ugh, I'm still so sore. But I'm getting better,' she added hastily as I moved away from her. I'd almost forgotten yesterday's ugly ordeal. Almost.

I still had no idea what I'd said that was so brilliant, but I trusted Ellie. She's got great instinct so I waited for her to explain. That, too, is a fairly predictable Ellie reaction: she's a natural-born teacher.

'Look,' she said, moving over to the corner desk and rummaging through the top drawer. Pulling out a pencil, she carefully began to scribble over the paper's surface. It reminded me of when my mother and her sister, Ellie's mom, would head out for a day of 'doing the graves', as they laughingly called it. They loved finding old and unusual headstones and would produce 'rubbings' from them, adding them to the copious bits of paper already in their collections. What Ellie was doing right now looked like the technique they used.

'Aha!' Ellie sounded as though she'd made the discovery of the century. I almost expected to hear her shout 'Eureka!'

I crowded close behind her, resting my chin gently on her shoulder. I looked at what she had uncovered, and it did look like a list. A list comprised solely of names.

You know when you have those moments of completely inspired thoughts, the kind that makes you all tingly and almost breathless? That was exactly how I felt in the instant that the light bulb went on: whoever it was that attacked Ellie had not been in here looking for Emmy's letter. They'd been looking for their list.

Chapter Nineteen

Ellie's careful rubbing managed to reveal several names: José Ramirez Rascon; Keith McClellan; Richard Olsen; Israel Martinez; Danny Martinez. I couldn't think what they might mean, but apparently the list was important enough for someone to almost kill Ellie.

'Is this anything we should call the police about? I mean, *I* think it's a lead, but would *they*?' I began pacing the room, arms wrapped around my waist and eyes on the ceiling as if the answer would suddenly appear, announced in flashing neon letters and accompanied by a fanfare. I knew Detective Fischer probably thought I was some kind of a nut, and I didn't want that idea planted anywhere else, i.e. in Detective Baird's mind.

Thoughts of Detective Baird reminded me that I hadn't seen him since Emmy's body had been discovered. I wondered if he'd been reassigned to some other case now the body count had stabilized. After all, we'd managed to downgrade action at the resort to a simple beating.

Wait – the attack on Ellie had been anything but simple. It was vicious and she might have died if we hadn't gotten to her. I shook my head to loosen the unaccustomed skepticism. That was Ellie's department. Besides, who could stay pessimistic with a dimpled smile hovering in their head? Not me!

'Look, AJ. Whether they think it's important or not, we need to call the police. I think you're right about what the intruder ...' Here Ellie's voice shook a bit '... was probably looking for. And I think if we tell them that, explain about the list, then they'll listen. Or at least they'll pretend to listen.'

She laughed the short cynical laugh she had whenever she was feeling negative about something.

I thought about it for a minute then nodded.

'Plus,' I said, sitting down on the edge of the bed and giving it a slight bounce, 'that explains Emmy's letter, if you think about it. If there really is some kind of identity fraud going on, maybe these names are the guys involved.'

It made so much sense to me, I almost laughed aloud. Detective Dimple had better watch his back: AJ and Ellie were on the case! For the first time in a few days, I felt like going out into the bright sunshine and enjoying what time I had left in San Blanco. Folding the list, I shoved it into my back pocket. Unless the Miramar had a pickpocket in addition to a killer, it should be safe.

Ellie was watching me and gave me on those looks that clearly said 'hold on there, pardner'. She was well-versed in my 'ready, fire, aim' tact, and had talked down many an issue for me that had been the disastrous result of that line of thinking. Although, come to think of it, I usually wasn't thinking, just instinctively reacting. Whatever. If it got the job done, who could find fault?

'What?' I asked her, ever the innocent. 'Do you want to get this thing over and done with or not?' This is another of my skills: dump the problem squarely back on whoever is playing Doubting Thomas, or in this case, Doubting Thomasina.

Ellie's reply was a well-timed eye roll. How well she knew me.

'Fine,' I said. I was ready to hit the sleuthing trail, or whatever it was called, and I wasn't keen on sitting in my room for one minute more. 'Let's get going, OK?' I folded my hands into their prayerful form. I wasn't above begging if I needed to.

'Hang on. I'm thinking.' Ellie closed her eyes. Great.

Now she was going to meditate us into catching the Miramar Murderer.

'You sit there and think, missy. I'm going to catch me a killer.' I acted like I was heading out the door. There was no reply from my cousin. She could smell an empty threat a mile off.

I gave up, plopping back down on the bed. 'Fine. Let's just sit here. Hopefully no one else will meet their doom,' I said dramatically, 'while you go into a trance.'

Ellie opened her eyes, a placid look on her face. I'd seen that look before. It meant 'I have a plan and you will go with it', or something along those lines. She could be so bossy!

On cue, as if she had just read my thoughts, she said, 'Assertive, AJ. I'm assertive. Not bossy.'

That spooked me, so I meekly followed her out of the bedroom and through the front door. I had no idea where we were headed, but for all intents and purposes, Ellie was now the leader, and I had been relegated to sidekick.

'First things first,' she announced, steering us toward the kitchen. I groaned to myself. I could already see what was coming: Ellie's groupies were going to get another visit from Her Highness, and I was going to get in some major trouble if we were caught in a 'Staff Only' area. After all, I didn't work here any longer – at least on the books – and I didn't want to get thrown out on my ear until we got a few things accomplished.

'Er ... Ellie?' I gripped her elbow, hoping to slow her down. She was already moving into her 'I mean business' mode. 'I don't think it's a good idea to ...'

She didn't let me finish. Instead, she shook off my hand and continued to stride purposefully down the corridor. Looking back over her shoulder, she merely said, 'Are you coming or what, AJ?'

As if I'd stay out here by myself! I began trotting, trying to keep pace with her. Wherever we were headed –

and I still had my money on the kitchen – Ellie was clearly on a mission.

Too bad we can't bet on ourselves, you know? I'd have won, hands down, on this one. Sure enough, we were once again in the kitchen, standing by the same counter with the same group of staff standing around, each with the same look of expectancy on their faces. Ellie Saddler, card reader *extraordinaire*, was about to reveal all. I just wanted her to hurry up, never mind the theatrics.

It grew silent, so silent, in fact, that I thought I could hear my heart reverberating, echoing throughout the expansive room. Or maybe that was just the blood pounding in my ears, indicating my blood pressure had spiked, a not-so-uncommon occurrence whenever Ellie was about. From the looks on the faces of those gathered around her, their blood pressures were up as well. In fact, one face in particular looked awfully flushed.

Fernando, apparently finding other things to do than valet the guests' cars, was standing close to Maria, his chin on her hair and both arms around her slim waist. Love was undeniably in the air, I mused. Maria must have felt my gaze on her because she shifted her eyes in my direction and gave me a shy smile. Well, better her than me, I thought. Ignorance was obviously a blissful state for some.

'Someone at the Miramar,' Ellie began, instantly reclaiming my full attention, 'is holding a secret. This secret is so important to them, so vital, that they are willing to kill for it.' A low murmuring began, but she held up her hand for silence.

'This person is involved in something not right, something illegal. It has brought happiness to some and death to others. But to this person, the secret-holder, it has brought untold riches. Because of this, they will gladly remove anyone they think is in their way.'

Ellie held up the card depicting The Fool, the one she'd shown to me.

'This is a picture of the killer. He may look innocent and harmless on the outside, even kind, but inside he is another person altogether. He will be caught, make no mistake about that. But until then, do not trust anyone.'

If a room can be described as 'deathly silent' – completely apt here – the Miramar's kitchen certainly was. No one said a word, instead looking at one other and back to Ellie with intense concern on their faces. I wasn't sure how much they actually understood, but they'd caught enough of the meaning to move soberly away from the counter and back to their tasks. Maria and Fernando stayed where they were, and I saw that Maria's eyes had filled with tears. Her brother's death was still so recent, her emotions still raw, and hearing Ellie talk about the killer had triggered renewed grief. I was thankful she could lean on Fernando, literally and figuratively.

Catching Ellie's eye, I motioned with my head toward the kitchen door. She nodded, moving away from the counter and past Maria. The girl, still silently weeping, caught at Ellie's arm with one slender hand as she walked past.

'Please, Miss Ellie. Can you tell me who it is?'

It was clear Maria thought Ellie had a name and was just keeping it to herself, and I watched curiously to see what Ellie would do. Knowing how she operated these things, she would only have an idea of what the person would be like, a sort of profile.

'I'm sorry,' she said gently, easing Maria's hand from her arm. 'I never see names, Maria, only what the person is like. You must be careful and not trust those around you, at least until this is over.'

Fernando's eyes had narrowed, and the previous redness in his face was now gone, replaced by a coolness that looked far from pleasant. Ellie was not making friends and influencing folks, I could see that. It was definitely time to take our leave, to get out while the gettin' was good.

'Er … Ellie, I need to get that paper to … er … to Stan as soon as possible,' I said, sounding like I'd made it up on the spot, which, of course, I had. Luckily, Ellie had a lot of experience in AJ-speak, so she merely nodded at me and moved in my direction. The sooner we were out of that kitchen, the better I'd feel.

Ellie headed for the door, leaving me to trail behind and give Maria and Fernando a weak smile of farewell. At this point, although I couldn't put my finger on it, I was pretty sure we'd chanced on something that could turn real bad real quick.

I caught up with Ellie outside the kitchen door. I could tell right away that she'd picked up on the weird vibes as well; her little speech about The Fool had clearly hit a nerve. I was in no doubt that Fernando was none too happy with either of us.

We didn't say a word until we'd started walking down the corridor toward the main lobby. I didn't have an obligation to check on the concierge desk, but force of habit turned my feet in that direction.

'So,' I began, casting a quick glance around the lobby. Stan West was sitting hunched over the desk, with a stack of folders in front of him. I gave Ellie a silent nod, indicating that now was a good time to sneak out before he saw us. Or, at least, before he saw me. I had this feeling that there was no love between us at the moment.

The morning breeze carried on it a hint of saltiness, and it reminded me of the jar of shells I'd had as a child. There is something about a combination of salt and that strange fishy smell that defines the seaside. Unfortunately, I'd probably always associate it with death and unhappiness from now on. I turned to Ellie, intending to finish my thoughts on Maria and the reading, when I heard a commotion.

With a sinking feeling, I watched Fernando as he

stormed toward us, Maria clutching ineffectually at his arm. I'd always heard of folks who, when faced with a traumatic ordeal, watch their lives flash before their eyes, but I'd never believed it – until now. My own life's movie reel was whirring along at top speed, my heart racing to keep pace. Ellie and I were sitting ducks.

Chapter Twenty

'Why are you accusing me of killing all these people?'

Fernando's words rattled at us like machine-gun shots and Ellie quickly stepped behind me, her eyes wide with fear. I was pretty scared myself, but it would do no good to go to my death shaking in my boots. I steeled myself, facing the raging bull head on.

With a scared-looking Maria hanging on his arm, Fernando stopped within inches of me, muscular arms crossed and eyes narrowed. Add his flaring nostrils to the mix, and the bull reference wasn't too far off base.

I could feel Ellie trembling as she stood close to me, and I got mad. Not mad enough to start something with Fernando, but mad enough to cross my own arms in a show of defiance. Where did this guy get off anyway, accusing us of ... well ... of accusing him?

'Unless you're calling yourself a fool, Fernando, Ellie wasn't talking about you.'

I felt a rush of adrenaline, something I'd probably need to help me run away as fast as I could. I'd just made Fernando even angrier, if that was possible. Way to go, big mouth, I thought grimly as I continued to exchange glares with him.

'Yeah, AJ's right, so what's the problem?'

That was Ellie, still tucked behind me but apparently feeling bold enough to add her two cents to the conversation. If we needed to take off running, though, it would be every man for himself. Or herself, in this case.

'So, if you're not talking about me, who is it then? Tell

me that!' Fernando tone was challenging and, although his nostrils had stopped their flaring, his body language still said 'very mad person standing here'.

Ellie stepped out from behind me, hands raised in a placating gesture. She acted like she was dealing with an unruly child, not a very large and furious man.

'Look, Fernando. My readings don't give me a particular name. It's never happened that way before and it probably won't start happening now.' She looked from Fernando to Maria. 'Maria, I told you that I could only tell you what the killer might do or say, not that I knew who it was.'

'That is so, Miss Ellie, but I thought that we could tell who it was by what you were saying. And the card you showed us, The Fool? That word, "fool", can make some people very, very angry.' She lifted her gaze to Fernando. 'Miss Ruiz, Emmy, she would get very mad at Fernando and call him a fool and other hurtful things. He thought maybe …' Her words trickled to a stop, and she leaned into Fernando's side, her hand resting protectively on his arm.

I recalled my first night at the Miramar, overhearing Emmy speak to Fernando in a tone that could be described as disparaging. No wonder he'd thought Ellie was talking about him! That was all he'd heard from Emmy, and the epithet still obviously stung.

Ellie took another step toward Fernando. Ellie is the family's resident 'hugger' and I was pretty sure she was going to give Fernando a squeeze. I could see he thought so as well, because he took one step backward and moved Maria in front of him before she knew what had happened, a look of something akin to panic on his broad face.

I almost laughed out loud. So the tough man was scared of something after all! Not that I could blame him; I'd seen Ellie in action too many times before to take her lightly.

We stood and watched Fernando and Maria walk back

to the resort hand in hand, his bulk making her look as small as a child beside him. I shook my head in wonder; I guess there really *was* someone for everyone, as Grandma Tillie was wont to say. Except for me, I added silently. Unless I got really lucky and Detective Baird suddenly found me irresistible, I was doomed to be alone.

I sighed, then turned to look at Ellie. Her gaze was fixed on something, and followed her line of sight. Stan West, the Miramar's general manager, stood just outside the lobby's doors, talking animatedly on a cellphone. With his gangly build and long arms, he looked like a large spider.

'You'd think he could keep his business private,' I commented as I watched him. So far he hadn't spotted us and I wanted to keep it like that, so I grabbed Ellie's arm and tugged her down the path toward the beach. I could use some fresh air and a place to hide out for a while.

We strolled down the sand a ways, shoes in hand and the breeze in our face. It was a pleasant day and it was hard to think that such a paradise had a more sinister side to it.

'So, Ellie,' I began, scooping up a broken shell and tossing it into the water, then glancing over my shoulder. 'If it's not Fernando, and I'm not saying that I ever thought it was, who do you think it could be?'

She shook her head slightly, one hand shielding her eyes from the sun. 'I'm not sure, AJ. Maybe one of those guys on the list we found.' She stopped walking and clapped one hand to her forehead dramatically. 'The list! We completely forgot to tell the detectives about it! We should probably do that ASAP, don't you think?'

I'd stopped walking as well; it's hard to carry on a conversation with someone ten feet behind you.

'I suppose,' I said doubtfully. 'Like I told you, we may think it's something but they might just think we're two nutcases from the boonies.'

'Well, it'd be pretty bad if we had the answer to the whole thing right in our hands and didn't share it. Besides,' added with a grin, 'there might be a reward or something.'

I hadn't considered that angle. I certainly could use an extra buck or two, so earning a reward of any size appealed to me. I grinned back at my cousin. Sometimes we *do* think alike.

'I'm game, Ellie. Nothing like filthy lucre for a little incentive.' I turned around.

'Race you back!'

With Ellie shrieking something about me cheating and how I never let her win anything – which was absolutely not true – we ran back to the Miramar, stopping to catch our breath as we approached the lobby. Stan West was nowhere in sight, which was a very good thing. Trying to maintain some air of propriety (there were a few guests still around, after all) Ellie and I strolled back to our suite.

I slid my key card through the reader and opened the door, to utter disaster. The front room looked like a tornado had moved through, with furniture on its side, cushions strewn about the floor, and a trail of clothes leading from the bedroom. I stood frozen to the spot, unable to move or speak. Words I'd heard before, a phrase someone had said about 'déjà vu all over again' flashed through my mind. We'd been visited again, it seemed, by the same person, or persons, who had attacked Ellie. Someone had either taken a chance on finding us at home, or they'd seen us leave.

And I had a sneaking suspicion which it was. We were on someone's radar.

Behind me Ellie gasped. Pushing past me into the suite, she looked around the room and then sank down weakly onto the couch. Instantly my distress switched from 'oh, my things are ruined' to concern with Ellie's state of mind. Her last run-in with the perp had ended rather badly for her, and this new intrusion was salt in the wound. I lowered myself gently beside her, careful not to brush against her still-bruised body.

'Ellie,' I said, 'it's OK. I'm here. No one is getting hurt this time around, I can promise you that.'

I patted her hands that lay clenched tightly in her lap, feeling inadequate, wanting to believe my own words of comfort. I needed something else, something that would calm the jitters of seeing my suite ransacked once again. Of course, you know what my go-to cure is, and I walked over to the phone to place an order for hot tea and fresh cookies. I was pretty sure that Stan wouldn't begrudge my cousin a first-aid treatment of the sugary kind. And if he did ... oh, well. He could deal with it.

My next decision was a tad more serious. I needed to call this latest incident in to the San Blanco PD. And I needed to share the list of names with someone who'd take it seriously. Reaching for the phone, I dialed the number for Detective Fischer.

Within thirty minutes, the dynamic detective duo of Fischer and Baird had arrived. By this time, Ellie had calmed down and I had all my ducks in a row. Besides telling them about the list and asking what they thought about Emmy's letter, I would also let them know that Fernando's actions had sounded alarm bells as well, at least for me. Ellie can be a bit soft-hearted at times, but I know when to call a spade a spade. And Fernando was looking decidedly spade-ish to me.

Per usual, my temperature did that weird hot-cold fluctuation when Detective Baird strolled in, but at least I was able to keep a grip on my dimple response issue. Of course, I did this by not looking directly at him but at a point just above his head, but 'needs must when the Devil drives', as Grandma Tillie would say. (I know – it never made any sense to me either, but hey! It sure sounds good.)

Detective Fischer, notebook balanced on his paunch, looked from me to Ellie and back again. By now I recognized the signs of 'get on with it' in Fischer-speak, so I cleared my throat and plunged in. If they laughed, then so be it.

'My room – our room – was broken into again, and Ellie and I think we know what they were looking for.' I watched as Detective Fischer jotted something down, then stood to his feet.

'Baird, get Forensics here pronto. We may just get lucky this time and find a useful print or two.'

I raised my eyebrows at Ellie, signaling my surprise that they hadn't gotten anything the last time through my suite. Maybe our suspect was a little smarter than I'd given him – or her – credit for, managing to turn over a hotel room without leaving any traces behind. All the more reason they needed to see the list.

I jumped to my feet as well. 'I have something else to show you, if you'll wait a sec.' I reached into my back pocket for the list of names. And froze – it wasn't there. Either I'd lost it or someone had taken it.

I'm fairly certain that the look on my face told it all. When my hand came out of my pocket without the promised 'something to show you', Detective Fischer's radar went on high alert.

'So they got it this time, did they?' He looked serious, and I could feel my heart beginning to beat a tattoo of fear. Now whoever it was knew that I'd seen the names, and maybe, just maybe, one of those names belonged to a killer.

I nodded, gulping back my panic. 'It was a list. Five names. I might be able ...'

I broke off. I closed my eyes and tried to picture the names as Ellie revealed each one. 'I know there's an Israel. And a Danny. I'm pretty sure they had the same last name.' I turned to look at Ellie for confirmation.

She nodded. 'Yes, the same name. I think, at least I'm fairly sure, that it was Martinez.'

I didn't miss the strange look that passed between the detectives. 'What?' I demanded. 'Did we miss something?'

Detective Baird, devastating dimple carefully tucked away, nodded after another silent conversation with his partner. 'We did a next-of-kin notification this morning. The person who was found on Miramar property a few days ago was identified as Israel Martinez.'

Well. It would seem that Ellie and I had been on to something, all right. I scrunched up my face as I tried to remember the other names.

Ellie spoke up suddenly. 'José Rascon. Definitely. And Keith Mc-something or other. There's one more, but I can't ... wait! It was Richard Olsen.' She looked mighty pleased with herself, and I could have hugged her. Sometimes her memory can be a bit, shall we say, cloudy, but this was a direct hit.

Detective Fischer wrote furiously in his notebook. Finally he looked up. 'Get Forensics here, Baird. I need to get these two young ladies moved out.' He turned to face me and Ellie. 'Get your things packed ASAP. I'm moving you to another room.' He made the announcement as if *he* were the resort's manager and not Stanley West.

Thinking about Stan made me remember his strange behavior earlier, and I hesitated. Was this something to share or would it make me look nuttier than I already felt? Before I could decide, my in-suite phone rang.

Chapter Twenty-one

Ellie and I started like two scared rabbits. Before I could get to the phone, though, Detective Fischer held up his hand.

'Answer the phone like normal,' he directed me. 'I'm going to put my ear up close to the receiver so I can hear what is said.'

I suppose it did make sense for him to listen in, considering that no one had ever called me here except Emmy and that spooky someone I'd privately dubbed the Miramar Murderer. Still, getting cozy around the phone with Detective Fischer made me a little nervous. I would have preferred ... well, you know what I wanted. And it wasn't a cookie, if you get my drift.

I nodded at him then took a deep breath to steady my nerves. 'Hello?'

The silence was deafening. I was positive I could sense breathing on the other end. I looked at Detective Fischer for direction. He merely nodded at me, so I took that as a signal to speak up again.

'Hello? Is anyone there?'

This time, my voice quavered just a tad, but it was enough to make the detective frown and shake his head at me. Great. I'd just given my hand away, letting the caller know I was scared. Well, dang it, I was! This whole cat and mouse game was getting on my nerves and, combined with Ellie's attack and the three deaths, I'd had it. 'Look! If there's someone there, you'd better speak up and make it snappy!' I was scared, sure, but I was also mad as a wet hen. I couldn't care less if my words made Detective Fischer irritated or not. In response, I got a dial tone from the phone and caterpillar brows from Fischer.

I hung up the phone, just daring the detective to say something. I think, though, he could tell how irked I was, because all he did was sigh loudly – shades of my mother when she's put out about something. Oh, well: I tried, and that was more than I could say for some folks.

'I don't think it's a good idea for us to stay here,' said Ellie suddenly. Detective Fischer and I looked at her, waiting for enlightenment. Maybe Ellie was having come of her psychic moments. And maybe she was just as frightened as I was.

Detective Fischer crossed his arms, leaning back against the kitchen table. 'What makes you say that?'

Ellie shook her head slowly as if freeing a thought that had gotten trapped. 'I'm not sure. I just don't feel …' She hesitated for a moment, reaching for the right word. 'I still feel like whoever it is can see us through the walls. Is that weird?' She looked up at me and the detective, the dark smudges under her eyes a little more pronounced than they had been.

I shivered. I knew what she meant. Even if the killer wasn't at the Miramar physically, he – or she – still seemed to know where we were. Talk about disturbing! This was even more uncomfortable than that first school dance Ellie and I had attended, forced to go, of course, by our well-meaning mothers. They had insisted that we just 'give it a whirl, you might like it', but Ellie and I had spent most of those excruciating two hours hiding out in the girls' powder room.

'Do you have somewhere else in mind?' It was Detective Baird, who had come back into the room unnoticed. That in itself was amazing to me, since I generally kept tabs on him whenever he was nearby.

Ellie nodded, another interesting turn of events. I had

fallen off her train of thought a while back and had no idea where it might be going.

'Why can't we stay with someone in the police department?'

I almost fell over. Really, Ellie? Although, now that I thought about it ... I grinned to myself, catching the twinkling baby blues of Detective Baird. Detective Fischer's eyebrows climbed nearly to his hairline. I could see that he was as bemused as I was and probably wondering how he could back out of his original suggestion.

'How about Packard's place? He and his wife have a spare room. Or maybe Annie? She's got space now that ... well, she probably has room for them.' Detective Baird's face split into a grin, and judging by the intense scowl on his partner's face, he had hit a nerve. Well, well, I thought with amusement. Still waters run deep and all that jazz. Who'd a thunk it?

'Yes, well, I'm sure she'd be OK with it. You call her, Baird. I need to get busy here.' With that, Detective Fischer stepped outside to speak with the forensics team who'd just arrived with their gear.

Detective Baird pulled out his cellphone and punched in a few numbers.

Ellie and I sat on the couch, she with her eyes closed and head resting against the cushions and me with my ears in strain mode, trying to hear his conversation. Unfortunately, Baird walked outside and I lost the gist of what he was saying. I'd just have to wait.

'OK, then. Sounds good. We'll be by in twenty,' said Detective Baird as he stepped back inside, checking his watch. 'OK, yep. Gotcha. Yep, no prob. See ya.' He snapped the cellphone closed and slipped it back into his pocket. 'Give Forensics a sec to check out the bedroom and bathroom, then you girls can pack and we'll get out of their hair. Sound good?' His smiled at the both of us, although I was pretty sure I could detect more dimple action when he looked at me.

Ellie nodded wearily. She did look bad today, I thought, and I wanted to get her moved and settled in as fast as possible. I dittoed her nod, then stretched my legs out in front of me in what I hoped was a languid manner. My knees made a loud popping noise, though, obliterating any chance of sensuousness I'd thought to achieve. I tell you what: if it's not my stomach giving me away, it's my body. A girl just can't win. I was playing to an audience of one anyway, and she still had her eyes closed.

Within a fairly short amount of time, the forensics folks had swept through the bedroom and bathroom, giving Ellie and me the nod to finish our packing. I carried both sets of luggage into the front room and joined Ellie on the couch again as we waited for the signal to move out. I could hear the two detectives talking just outside the door and it sounded like a one-sided conversation to me, with Fischer trumping whatever it was Baird was trying to get across. I grinned to myself. I just loved hearing a handsome man taking orders.

Detective Annie Bronson's house, a cute little bungalow set square in the middle of a handkerchief-size patch of grass, was about ten miles further down the coast. Here the sea looked choppier and the skies weren't as blue, as though they'd had all the color wrung out of them. Still, living near water of any kind has always appealed to me, and I was glad that Detective Bronson was willing to take on the two of us as impromptu guests.

A short blonde with a curvy figure, Annie, as she told us to call her, hovered just this side of fifty, making it look like an easy job. Granted, she had the tell-tale wrinkles of the outdoor enthusiast, and her skin was a tad too tanned for my taste, but all in all, I could see the attraction factor for Detective Fischer. I could afford to feel magnanimous; Detective Baird, it would appear, was just her friend and nothing more.

Ellie and I settled into a back bedroom just off the main hallway. Its two windows looked out over a backyard full of color; riotous bougainvillea spread its tendrils along the length of a wooden fence as other flowers jostled one another for space in the beds below. I envied Annie this paradise, but I guess there's really no place like home. Memories of pine trees and creeks and soft snow flurries filled my mind, and I felt a twinge of something akin to homesickness. Boy, I really *was* getting soft, especially since I'd willingly traded said homestead for the beach ... and a killer.

'Make yourselves at home, gals.' Detective Bronson – oops, I mean Annie – opened the closet near her front door and reached in for a light jacket. 'I'll be gone for about an hour, maybe two, but if you need anything just call my cell. I left the number on the fridge.' With a smile like morning sunshine, she breezed out through the door.

I wandered through the house, picking up the various knick-knacks and thumbing through the books that seemed to be on every available surface. Her taste ran to mysteries – no surprise there – and I saw that she read many of the same authors I did: P.D. James; Elizabeth George and the like. What I didn't understand was this: if we had the same taste in books, how in the world had she been able to feel romantic over someone like Detective Fischer? Weird.

I was standing in the front room, staring out the picture window when movement outside caught my eye. A man stood there, leaning against the fence surrounding the yellow house across the street. The dark wrap-around sunglasses and his stance, arms crossed and chin jutting out, gave me goose bumps. If he was waiting for someone, he didn't look at all happy.

Ellie came up behind me, resting her chin on my shoulder. I craned my neck to look at her, smiling to see her more relaxed than she had been in a few days.

'Hey, kiddo,' I said, turning my head back to watch the man. He had moved a bit further out onto the sidewalk, talking on a cellphone held between his shoulder and jaw, gesticulating with one hand. He was definitely looking angry.

Suddenly he spun around and stared straight at us. Ellie gasped and shrank back, but I felt frozen to the spot, unable to move. The now-familiar shivers played up and down my spine as I watched him watching me. Was I looking at the Miramar Murder?

I was distracted by the sound of a motor revving and screeching tires as a low-slung truck veered around the corner and slammed to a halt in front of the man, effectively blocking my view. The driver leaned across the seat and said something through the open passenger window, then looked over his shoulder at Annie's house. By this time, my heart had begun to climb its way from my chest into my throat. With everything that had happened so far, I was seeing threats everywhere, On the other hand, he could simply be a resident ...

'I think we need to call Detective Bronson,' said Ellie, interrupting my thoughts, her voice a strained version of its normal self. 'This is getting ridiculous, AJ.'

I couldn't have said it better myself. For whatever reason, someone – very possibly one of the men outside – had it in for Ellie and me. If it was the list of names, then that was out of our hands – literally. If it was something they thought we knew, I couldn't do squat about that. However, I could – and would – make sure that we weren't a sitting target. I turned to look at my cousin.

'Ellie, you get Annie on the phone. I'm calling in the big boys.'

My fingers felt twice their normal size, and I couldn't keep them steady enough to dial the phone. Finally, completely frustrated with myself and ticked off at the entire craziness of it all, I threw down my cell and marched out to the kitchen. I was relieved to see a normal-sized phone hanging on the wall near the back door and walked over to grab the handset.

    Just as I my fingers closed over the cool plastic, a sound from just the other side of the door made me jump ten feet into the air. My heart, of course, had already beaten me to it and was now dangling somewhere above my head. A slight exaggeration, I know, but that's exactly how it felt. I had never been so scared in all my life. *Again.*

Chapter Twenty-two

I'm not too sure what I was thinking at that moment, but I dropped to the floor and made myself as small as possible against the linoleum. From the corner of my eye, I could see Ellie's feet as she came around the doorway and stopped abruptly.

'Get down, get down!' I hissed, motioning at her. She obediently crouched down, peering around the corner and making wild hand gestures back at me. If I had to guess, she'd just used some unprintable words.

If this had been a spy thriller, Ellie and I would be the agents in the crosshairs of the enemy. With that comforting thought, I began edging toward the hallway where Ellie was, moving turtle-style across the floor. My only hope at that moment was that whoever was on the other side of that door wouldn't think to look down when he peeked through the curtainless window.

Ellie and I stayed huddled together while she whispered to Annie Bronson on the other end of the line. I still had the phone's handset, but my fingers were shaking too badly to dial anything, even a number as simple as 911. I can completely understand how someone can feel petrified with fear and not be able to move away from a dangerous situation.

Ellie stuck her head close to mine and whispered, 'Annie's on her way and so are your detective buddies.' I gave her an irritated shove; they were not *my* anything.

Another thud against the back door made us both jump and clutch at each other. When we were much younger (and much smaller), Ellie and I seemed to attract trouble like a magnet does metal shavings. Once, on a dare, we'd slipped into old Mr Jenkins' house, a run-down, dilapidated excuse for a building. I can't remember the specifics, but the upshot is that we found ourselves cornered in a dark living room by a very angry Mr Jenkins, whose threats of running us in to the local police station had us sniveling and crying like two babies. While I didn't exactly feel like crying right now, I did feel trapped and scared. It's weird how the more things change, the more they stay the same.

Sometimes I get these "wild hairs", as my mother refers to them, and do things that I can't rationally explain. That would definitely apply to what I did next. Disentangling myself from Ellie's grasp, I went into military mode and belly-scooted my way into the front room, heading straight for the window. Ellie was almost hysterical behind me, hissing warnings and sounding for all the world like a snake under great stress. I ignored her, something I've perfected over the years, and found myself just under the window's ledge. I really didn't have a plan for my next move – typical for someone who lives life on the fly – but it occurred to me that I'd have to raise my head above the sill in order to peer out. Eyes on the top of my head would have been perfect.

I was saved from having to make this decision by the sound of several cars pulling up all at once. I hoped this meant the cavalry had arrived. If not, Ellie and I were definitely outnumbered. The squawk of police scanners could be heard and I nearly kissed the floor with happiness when the sound of a key turning in the front door reached my ears.

'Are you two OK?' Annie's concerned voice came from somewhere above my head and I slowly rose to my feet, still a bit wary of exposing myself to whoever was outside the window. 'AJ? Ellie?'

'In here,' I said weakly as Ellie called out from the hallway where she'd remained until certain of safety.

I could hear movement from all around the small house now and voices of various officers calling to one another as they cleared each area. I was starting to feel embarrassed, like maybe we'd jumped the gun over this whole thing, and that our nerves had convinced us that trouble was about. I was just trying to find the words to formulate an apology with when I heard a sudden shout and sounds that indicated convergence at one particular spot in the backyard. My heart rate picked up a bit in anticipation of being exonerated, albeit in my own mind. I hate to look like a fool.

Ellie walked into the front room where I still stood, watching two rather large police officers patting down the two men who'd spooked us. The driver of the truck was leaning against his vehicle, legs spread and hands placed flat on the truck's hood, while the other man, the scary-looking one who had been on his cellphone, was being held against the other side, yapping a mile a minute at the officer checking him for weapons, or whatever it is they look for in a pat-down. To the officer's credit, he kept his cool, responding minimally, all the while doing his job. That is one profession that has my profound admiration. Well, that, and teaching high school. They both seem to tread boldly where even the angels fear to go.

Beside me, Ellie gave a little shudder as she slipped her arm through mine. 'What do you think will happen with those two?' she asked, pointing with her chin across the street.

I knew what she was thinking, and I agreed: I didn't want them out and about, not if they had anything to do with the Miramar issues. I shrugged, trying to project 'casual and unconcerned'. No need for the two of us to be upset.

Annie Bronson came back inside. She left the kitchen

door wide open, and I could clearly hear voices as each officer examined something lying on the ground just off the back steps. I was dying to get out there and poke around, but figured I'd better stay put, at least for the moment. I wanted to be seen as an asset, not someone in the way. Unless Detective You-Know-Who was acting as a human blockade. Then I might consider ...

Reality check, AJ, I chided myself. Let's just work on solving this issue first before we jump into any more hornets' nests, OK?

'Here's the scoop,' announced Annie as she pocketed a notebook. 'The two jokers across the street swear they have no idea why they've been stopped, but one of them is carrying an ID that claims that his name is John Smith, while the other's license identifies him as John Kuscak. Not too original with the first names, that's for sure,' she chuckled.

Ellie and I stared at one another without a word. I could tell that Ellie was as baffled as I was; I mean, lots of folks are called John, right? I glanced outside as the men were each put in the back of a police cruiser, hands cuffed behind them and furious scowls on their faces. Whatever they were being taken in for, they were mad as two hornets themselves!

'Well,' said Annie abruptly, consulting the very large wristwatch on her right arm, 'If I'm going to be in on this I need to get going.' She looked at Ellie and me as if we knew what she was talking about. Our expressions must have spoken volumes because she stopped, hands on hips and an amazed look on her face.

'For some reason, I thought you two knew about ... well, never mind. We just picked up two guys with fake IDs. And that's just scratching the surface. Whoever was here ...' she indicated the backyard with her chin '... they weren't the friendly type. We found a loaded pistol kicked in a corner by the back steps. It'll be printed and logged as evidence, and I have a feeling that one of those sweeties out there ...' here a chin jerk toward the front of the house '... had something to do with this.'

I don't know who felt more stunned at Annie's bombshell announcement, me or Ellie. I knew that eventually all of this would start making sense, and now I could see how Emmy's concerns, the list of names, and Maria's fears were all viable reasons to be afraid of these people. This was a lucrative trade, the fake ID card business, especially in a resort area where jobs were plentiful for those who possessed identification. I could understand why some would take the risk, but I still couldn't fathom losing my life over it. That just went to show how little I knew about the desperation of these folks.

I plopped down on the nearest chair, an IKEA model with a bouncy wooden frame and minimal padding. Pulling my feet into the seat, I wrapped my arms around my knees and sat silent. I needed to process all that had happened since we'd arrived at Annie's bungalow, and wondered if Ellie regretted the suggestion to leave the Miramar.

'I did another reading,' Her matter-of-fact tone belied the seriousness of what Ellie had just announced. I knew her well enough to realize she was sufficiently bothered about current events to react this way; she did not use her cards for personal gain or answers.

'And?' I raised one eyebrow at her in question.

Ellie looked down at her hands. 'I'm not sure, AJ. The cards have never been so ... well, so obscure. I can't see anything.' She lifted her head, a sober look on her face. 'I'm really scared, AJ.'

'I am too, Ellie, but we'll get through this. The police are taking care of things now and we're safe here, OK?' Not that I believed it without a 24/7 police guard but I knew Ellie was looking for comfort.

She gave a snort, accompanied by one of her trademark eye rolls. 'Right. Look how safe we were today,' she said sarcastically.

I shot her an irritated look. 'Ellie, it wasn't my idea to leave the Miramar.'

Oops – I'd just fired off an unintended first salvo. Not a wise move when dealing with Ellie; she was Queen of the Word Wars, and I usually backed off quickly, choosing the role of loser rather than 'walking wounded'. I attempted to back-pedal as I watched her eyes narrow and lips fold tightly together. She was gearing up for a return shot when my cellphone rang.

'This is AJ,' I answered, the words 'saved by the bell' traipsing through my brain. My cousin, thwarted by technology, could only mutter to herself. I smiled at her as I half-listened to Annie Bronson. Ellie glowered back. Typical, but she'd get over it. Eventually.

Suddenly Annie's words made me forget the potential feud and sit up straight. 'Say that again?' I asked, opening my eyes wide.

'One of those *gentlemen* we arrested today, and I do use that term loosely, was identified as Danny Martinez, the brother of the guy found at the Miramar last week. Since that was one of the names on the list you so kindly shared with Fischer and Baird, I thought you'd like to know.'

'Really,' I replied, sounding inane but, honestly, what else could I say?

I could hear someone talking in the background, and Annie said abruptly, 'OK. I need to go, AJ. Stay in the house and I'll be there about five.' With that, the line went dead.

'Well?' Ellie sounded impatient, as if I'd withheld some important info from her. 'They've identified another person from the list.'

Ellie just stared back. 'Who?'

'Israel Martinez's brother. Danny Martinez. Remember? Israel was the first body they found at the Miramar?'

'Ah,' Ellie said, sounding sage.

'"Ah", what?' I was beginning to get irked at her abstruse and monosyllabic responses, especially since she'd just been ready to annihilate me five minutes before.

'That explains what I saw in the cards,' she replied, standing to her feet and stretching, arms raised high over her head.

'You just told me that the cards didn't say squat, Ellie,' I said, feeling exasperated. 'Now you say you saw the Martinez brothers?'

She began walking toward the kitchen, but turned to give me a superior smile. 'I saw them last night.' With that parting shot, she walked out of the front room, leaving me fuming.

Chapter Twenty-three

If there is anything more irritating than carrying on an argument with the back of someone's head, I don't know what it is. Ellie knows that, just like she knows all the other buttons to push with me. I have to admit, though, that she is as loyal as the day is long and would gladly tear off someone's head if they said anything rude about me. With that in mind, I let it – and Ellie – go.

I sat and stared out the window, not really seeing anything. I felt so far removed from the Miramar and my job as an assistant concierge, and it felt like months since I'd done any real work. Sighing, I leaned my head back and let my eyes fall shut. Sleep was my weapon of choice whenever things went belly up in my life, and I was beginning to feel like a good hibernation might be the order of the day.

When my cell rang once more, I was tempted not to answer. It would either be Detective Annie Bronson with another update – she could just leave a message – or, heaven forbid, my mother, whose sixth sense for all things catastrophic rivals Ellie's. I couldn't help glancing at the screen, though, curious to see which one it was. The name that appeared surprised me, enough to actually answer.

'What?' I said curtly into the phone.

'Get in here,' hissed Ellie, speaking so close to the mouthpiece that it sounded like static coming through the lines.

'Why?' I whispered back, feeling a trifle silly. I mean, she *was* in the next room.

'I think there's someone in the house, AJ! Get in here now!' Ellie disconnected and I sat, phone in hand, staring at the blank screen. What in heaven's name was going on now?

Heart pounding – the last week had done wonders for my cardio health, blood pressure notwithstanding – I slid from my chair and crouched on the floor, now conscious of the sounds around me. With my ears tuned to radar-detection strength in order to hear what Ellie had heard, I half-walked, half-crawled into the kitchen. Ellie was under the table, and why she thought that was such a great hiding spot I had no idea. She was clearly visible from the hallway and I almost laughed out loud when I saw her.

Sliding under the table's edge, I sat on the floor next to her. She really looked scared, and I impulsively hugged her.

'Ellie, old houses make noise. Maybe that's what you heard, you know?' I squeezed her, feeling her shoulders tremble under my arm.

'I know what old houses do and don't do, thank you very much.' The old Ellie was back, quick as a flash, which took care of the shaking. I had to smile. She is so wishy-washy sometimes. 'Just listen for a sec.'

I felt like a participant in one of the old 'duck and cover' videos the Government used to put out during the Cold War years. Instead of listening for incoming atomic bombs, though, I was listening for an intruder in a house that wasn't mine, kind of like a pot calling a kettle black.

'How are the mighty fallen,' I muttered to myself, earning a sharp jab of Ellie's bony elbow. If this kept up, I would be black and blue.

A loud creak from the hallway made me jump, literally, and I whacked the top of my head. There was an instant silence. Ellie's eyes grew so large I thought she'd lose an eyeball, and my pulse seemed to migrate from my chest to my head. I was fully scared to death. That was becoming the emotion *du jour* here in San Blanco.

'See? I told you!' Ellie triumphantly sprayed the words across my face and I gave her a dark look in return as I wiped them from my cheeks. Nothing like an impromptu shower, courtesy of my hissing cousin.

Before I could think of something equally childish to say, a soft sound, almost a sigh, could be heard clearly from the hallway. It was vaguely familiar, although I couldn't place it. Apparently Ellie could, and did: she leapt from beneath the table and made a mad dash for the back door, with me hot on her heels and my heart pounding to beat the band.

The sound of a bullet zinging past my ears gave me wings and I flew through the backyard and all but vaulted the low wall in one mighty jump. Ellie was close behind and we fell, panting and staring at each other, into the empty lot behind Annie's house. I couldn't hear anyone chasing us, so maybe the bullet was just a friendly reminder to keep our noses out of someone's business. Someone's very illegal, very lucrative business.

The snapping of twigs and the thud of heavy feet on the ground shook me to life.

Grabbing Ellie by the hand, I tugged her to her feet and we sprinted for the nearest house, a small cottage on the edge of the vacant lot that hugged the edge of the water.

Please, oh please, oh please, let someone be there, I silently begged. Preferably someone with a phone and a hefty lock on the front door and bulletproof windows.

I chanced a look back over my shoulder and saw the top of someone's head as they peered over the fence. When an arm came over the top, something shiny in hand, I pulled Ellie to the ground and began scooting crab-like through the lot.

'Hey! What's going on? You there!'

I was never so glad to hear someone shouting at me. Standing near the back door of the small house stood a woman whose size belied the toughness of her words. When I saw the shotgun in her hand, I felt both relieved and worried; I didn't want the little old lady from San Blanco to take a potshot at me just as I was escaping a killer.

'It's OK, it's OK!' I shouted back, getting back to my feet and heading for her house. In response, she raised the shotgun to shoulder height. Ellie and I waved frantically at her, yelling that we were running from someone who'd taken a shot at us. To my intense relief, she lowered the weapon.

Panting and covered with dust from our crawl through the lot, Ellie and I stumbled into the woman's yard. I turned to look back toward Annie's house and saw the figure of a man standing in the spot where Ellie and I had landed when we vaulted the fence. I pointed.

'Look! There he is!' The woman craned her neck and squinted slightly, her eyes narrowed against the sunlight.

Ellie was on her feet and running before I could stop her. She headed straight for the door of the little house and burst inside. I shrugged an apology and made to follow, but the old lady reached out and grabbed my arm as I passed. Her grip was strong, and I had no choice but to stop.

'What's going on, young lady?' she demanded, a suspicious look crossing her face.

'We're trying to get away from him.' I gestured over my shoulder at the man who was now walking away toward the front of Annie's property. The woman followed his movements with her eyes then turned loose of my arm.

'You might as well go inside. Seems your friend's already made herself at home.' The grin instantly softened the pattern of wrinkles that ran through her face, giving her a kindly, grandmotherly look. Of course, I've never seen a grandmother who carried a shotgun around, but there's always a first.

I smiled at her gratefully. Any port in a storm, I always say, and this particular port came with its own armory, making me feel a tad better about being chased. At least the playing field was closer to level now, thanks to a gun-totin' granny.

The inside of her cottage was – no other word for it – eclectic, to say the least. Antiques jostled for space with stacking plastic cubes that held books of every kind, and the mishmash of patterns that assailed my eyes almost made me dizzy. In short, it looked perfect for someone like her.

'Name's Sarah Bacon, but I never use it. Call me Sal,' she said, stumping over to the sink and running water into a kettle that looked as old as she was. The gun was still tucked under an arm, and I began to wonder if it was some sort of accessory, a good luck charm of sorts. She must have read my thoughts because she said, 'It isn't loaded. Just use it for scaring folks who have no business on my property.'

I smiled at her in what I hoped was a friendly manner, but my mouth was so dry from running that I could feel my lips stretching across my teeth. I'm sure I looked as feral as I felt. 'We didn't mean to invade your space, ma'am.'

'Well, you did,' Sal said bluntly. 'And your friend there,' she added, pointing with her chin at Ellie who sat curled on one end of a couch covered with violently-colored flowers, 'She just came in without as much as a by-your-leave. Good thing I only use my gun for looks.'

Talk about jumping out of the frying pan and straight into the fire! Ellie and I appeared to have stumbled into a time warp of sorts, with a woman whose words, demeanor and actions would be more at home in the mountains of the last century.

I was trying to think of another plan when Sal spoke up again.

'If you're running from those men, the ones who make a living out of cheating honest folks, with their false papers, and promises that are even more false, you're in a world of hurt. If I were you, I'd plan on lyin' low for a while. You can stay here if you need to. I could use the company and you could use a safe house.'

I figured that staying here, even for just a few hours, would be better than trying to get about on our own. At least we'd be with someone who actually knew how to handle a firearm and wasn't afraid to try. I had to smile. It was almost funny, in a weird way, to think that Detective Annie Bronson had her very own vigilante living less than a hundred yards away.

I looked straight into Sarah Bacon's shrewd eyes and said, 'We'd surely appreciate it.'

And then it occurred to me that she knew who we were running from, and why – she'd said as much. Things were getting "curiouser and curiouser", as Alice would say, and I was starting to feel as if Ellie and I were falling down our own rabbit hole.

Two mugs of tea and an hour later, I was sufficiently calmed down to tell Sal exactly what had transpired between accepting my dream job at the Miramar and this afternoon. It was the stuff of movies, I know, but all true and all too fresh in my mind. If someone had told me I'd be as close to death as I had been in the last few days, I'd have laughed them out of town. I wasn't laughing any more, though.

Sal stared at me thoughtfully, cradling her own mug as she eased back and forth in a rocking chair that looked like it belonged in a museum. She'd listened to me in silence, only interrupting for an occasional clarification. I had found myself talking to her as easily as I talked to my own grandmother. If my Grandma Tillie had carried a shotgun, they could have been twins. They both had that no-nonsense, take-care-of-business attitude that tended to make me spill my guts.

And now that I think about it, that's probably how my mother found out some things that I thought were my deepest, darkest secrets. Thanks for nothing, Grandma Tillie.

All talked out, we three sat in the darkening room, the squeak of the rocking chair punctuating the silence. I was still worried but not nearly as much as I had been. The problem had been handed over to someone whose existence I hadn't even been aware of a few hours before. Sal Bacon seemed more than capable of coming up with a plan and I was more than happy to let her.

Ellie was still curled up in a corner of the couch. I was happy to see that her movements were more natural, not so stiff, and that her bruises were fading. I'd seen Sal looking at them but she'd asked nothing. Hopefully she'd put two and two together and gotten 'running from a crazy person' and not something more sinister. Although, come to think about it, that was sinister enough in itself.

'OK, girls. This is what I think we need to do.' Sal's abrupt announcement jerked me back to the present, and even Ellie perked up a bit. 'I've got enough supplies down cellar to outlast anyone trying to flush us into the open.'

I almost fell over. Number one, who even says 'down cellar' any more and number two, who has one?

'What do you mean, "flush us out into the open"?' I was rapidly moving from confident to concerned, with Sal sounding even more like that homespun vigilante than someone who could help.

'I think we just need a phone, Sal,' piped up Ellie. At last! A suggestion that didn't smack of conspiracy.

'I've got a phone you can use,' Sal countered, jerking a thumb toward a darkened room just off the front door. 'It's one of those satellite contraptions. Got it when I thought I'd have to hunker down during an enemy invasion.'

Oh, boy. We'd gone from running from a killer to

hanging out with a nutcase survivalist.

Could it get any worse? The answer, unfortunately, turned out to be a resounding 'Yes'.

Chapter Twenty-four

I just managed to keep myself from gawking at Sal. Who in their right mind would prepare for an 'enemy invasion' and install a satellite phone? Or even think about invasions of any kind? (I think the key words there are 'right mind'.) I was beginning to wonder what else she might have 'down cellar' aside from food. Visions of barricaded doors and night vision goggles danced through my already boggled mind; instead of planning how to escape killers, I needed a plan to escape from kooky old women.

You know how some folks can surprise you, no matter how well you think you know them? Dear Ellie managed to do just that.

'Let's get that phone hooked up, Sal,' said Ellie, rising to her feet and stretching. She'd sat still for so long – probably in recovery mode – that she was probably stiff as a board. Thankfully, her mind was still working. At least, I hoped it was, especially since she'd disappeared into the office of a crazy woman, alone and unarmed. I debated following them in there, wondering if I should stay close to the door in case I needed to make a break for it. Finally, with one last lingering look at potential freedom, I rose from my seat and walked into a center of technological wonder.

I've seen made-for-television movies where an average citizen becomes the hero of the day, defending the town against an alien invasion – the kind where all the houses are flattened by laser; except for the hero's house, of course.

I'm dead serious: the woman had a virtual armory of stockpiled guns in cabinets and hanging on the wall, an impressive shelving unit containing boxes of ammunition and goggles that looked like the night vision variety, and a desk that looked like the master command center for the CIA. In short, Sal Bacon was ready for Armageddon.

I just wanted to get in touch with San Blanco Police Department. Hopefully they'd already started searching for us – at least I trusted they had.

Ellie had already settled into the impressive leather chair that sat at the desk, switching on buttons and powering up the biggest cellphone I'd ever seen in my life. Sal was flipping switches on a computer that sat on one side of the desk, syncing it to a hand-held device she casually pulled out of her shirt pocket. I shook my head in amazement: I'd never seen such a set-up in anyone's house. Actually, I'd only seen things like this on the cable military channel and in those movies where there's always an on-the-run ex-spy who's been wrongly accused of some terrible crime and the government is out to get him. Maybe Sal had more of a past than I thought.

'OK, it's working,' announced Ellie. She turned to look at me. 'AJ? Do you want to call Annie or shall I?'

Actually, I'd thought of calling our dynamic detective duo, especially since I hadn't had my Detective Baird fix for the day. 'How about Detective Fischer?' I suggested with my best innocuous look. I should have saved it.

With a masterful eye roll, Ellie passed me the phone. 'Go ahead. Give your Detective Dimple a call, AJ.' As I took the monster device from her, I stuck out my tongue. Sometimes that feels so good, you know?

Crediting my near-photographic memory – or an obsession with a certain dimpled detective – I punched in the number to Baird's cellphone. By the third ring, I was feeling slightly anxious. When his voicemail picked up, I disconnected. I wasn't positive about police protocol and all that, but it seemed to me that they had to remain available.

I shrugged my shoulders at Ellie, handing back the phone to her. She took it without a word and dialed quickly, calling Detective Annie Bronson, I assumed.

'Er ... Annie? This is Ellie, Ellie Saddler. Yes, that Ellie.' I could hear Annie's voice faintly and from the look on Ellie's face, something was off. 'OK, we'll stay put. No, we're all right.' Here she glanced over at Sal with a questioning look, who returned it with a nod. 'We're at Sarah Bacon's house, the one just behind yours ... yep, that's the one. You do, huh? Well, is that so?' Ellie smiled at Sal whose face wrinkled back at her mischievously. I had a sudden sneaking suspicion that Sal and Annie were old acquaintances.

After Ellie hung up, she turned on Sal, hands on hips. 'You are one tricky lady, Sal. Why didn't you tell us that you were ex-PD? And that you were Annie's aunt?'

I must confess, with deep apologies to my mother, that my mouth almost unhinged, falling open to its full extent. This whole thing was just getting weirder by the minute.

Sal gave a deep chuckle. 'Yep, guilty as charged. Annie got into the business because of me. I raised the girl and she always wanted to do whatever her Auntie Sal was doing. And I must say, she does one heck of a job.' She looked at me and then back to Ellie. 'So, are we all set for the time being?'

I exchanged shrugs with Ellie. It seemed we'd be as safe here as any other place, and I admit I was feeling better about the whole 'crazy lady with guns' thing.

'Sure, we're good.' I answered for both of us.

In addition to having her own arsenal, Sal had an awesome food supply as well. With me and Ellie ensconced in the cozy front room, she bustled around in her kitchen, slicing vegetables and dumping them into a simmering pot of seasoned chicken stock. When she pulled rolls from the fridge and began brushing them with melted butter, I almost swooned. I am a bread person through and through, and I could eat a dozen hot buttered rolls by myself. I'd need to watch my manners.

'So,' I ventured, ready to hear some old tales on Annie. 'How did Annie come to live with you?'

Sal was silent a moment and I felt awkward, hoping I hadn't offended her. She still had all those weapons, after all. Wiping her hands on her shirt, Sal leaned back against the kitchen sink.

'Well, her daddy was my youngest brother. I felt like his mama most of the time, and when he left home, he moved in with me. Eventually, I lost him to Annie's mother, some young thing he met over at the university. They eloped, had Annie, and died in a car crash when she was still a baby. I'm the only family she's ever known, really.' Sal cleared her throat gruffly. 'But I've always felt blessed to have had her in my life and my home. Like I said, she always copied me, determined to do everything I did. I was so proud the day she joined the force.' Sal's face was soft with the memory. With a small sigh, she turned back to her cooking.

'Darn it!' Ellie's words cut short the moment. 'My cards, AJ. I left them behind at Annie's.'

She was worried about her *cards*? I was concerned about escaping with my *life*!

'Really, Ellie? Your flippin' cards? What good have they done us so far?' Oh, boy. Open mouth, insert foot, AJ.

To my surprise, Ellie smiled. I mean it – she truly smiled at me, even after I'd committed the unforgivable and had insulted her beloved deck of cards.

'I know. But, AJ, you've got to admit that they have given us some guidance.' Ellie sat examining her perfectly groomed cuticles as if she'd just spotted a hangnail.

'Whatever,' I answered stubbornly. 'They made

Fernando mad at us, and that's about all.'

Sal waded into our little exchange then, probably heading off a huge argument.

Ellie and I can have some doozies.

'Are you talking playin' cards here, girls, or some other kind?' She sounded curious, and Ellie ate it up like a starving man on a Christmas ham.

'My Tarot cards, Sal,' Ellie said with a touch of pride in her voice. Good grief. To hear her talk, you'd think she invented the darn things. 'I use them to help folks, to give them answers.'

OK. I'd had about enough of her sanctimonious attitude. It was time to kick some Tarot tail here.

'What Ellie really means, Sal,' I said with my sweetest voice and smile, 'is that she uses the cards to butt into others' problems and make them even worse.' Now I'd done it, but I didn't care. I was feeling reckless. In one short week I'd faced death and disaster, and I could handle Ellie. Or so I thought.

If steam could really issue from someone's ears, Ellie would have been able to power her own engine at that moment. I'd pushed the one button that could really set her off; questioning her motives. Ellie fancies herself as a people's person, a true humanitarian, and I suppose she is. I mean, she was usually the one to talk to the new students, to welcome the odd person out to our lunch table. I always wondered why she did it, though, especially since she was also the first to start a tiff with anyone who crossed her.

Sal turned a stern face on me and I felt like I'd time-traveled back to Grandma Tillie's house when Ellie and I would be scolded for fussing.

'I'm sorry, Ellie. I guess I'm just tired of this whole thing.' I gave my cousin a rueful smile and, thankfully, she smiled back. War averted.

'It seems to me that the both of you have had a few rough days,' Sal said, moving to the cabinets and taking down three bowls 'Come and get some grub. Food always makes folks feel better.'

I couldn't have agreed more. By the second hot roll I felt much better, and by the end of the meal, I could have gladly flipped the cards for Ellie and would have been delighted to do so. Sal's chicken vegetable soup was magic.

Chapter Twenty-five

The shadows that had huddled in the corners of the front room began to move inward, and I was surprised to see the glint of a superb sunset outside the windows.

We'd eaten and cleaned the small kitchen, chatting as if we'd known each other all our lives.

Aunt Sal, as I'd come to think of her, was amazing. Her stories of the early years on the police force, just one of three women on the beat, left me filled with appreciation that I'd never had to experience a boss or peers like she'd had. I couldn't imagine being treated as if I were a second-class citizen, all because of a few chromosomes that had been left to chance.

Thinking of bosses led my thoughts to Stan West and I grinned to myself, wondering how that gentleman was getting along. As much as I'd have liked him to have an issue or two to deal with, I knew he'd most likely shovel it over his shoulder at folks like Maria.

I glanced idly around the room, my eyes falling on a squat bookcase that hugged a darkened corner. It was filled to overflowing with books of every shape and size, and I was curious what a woman with Sal's eclectic lifestyle would read. Curiosity being one of my stronger points, I stood up and walked over to the shelves, plopping myself down on the floor in front of them.

Within five seconds my alarm bells had begun to ring, and another ten seconds passed before I registered the form standing behind me. Aunt Sal leaned over and touched my shoulder, making me jump sky high.

'Surprising, ain't it?' Her voice was amused, and I craned my neck to look up at her. 'Surprising' wasn't the word I'd have chosen. Maybe 'unbelievable' or 'mind-boggling', since that's exactly how I saw the situation, certainly not a mere 'surprising'.

'Yes, it sure is ... "surprising",' I agreed, turning back to the shelf just in front of me. The titles almost screamed at me: "Thinking Critically" by Drs Evans and Galas; "Knowing Your Mind and Theirs" written by Samuel Johnston, PhD; "Turning Their Reaction into Action" by F. Bacon, M.S.

That last author made me stop and consider. Was this a Bacon family member, as in Sal Bacon? I must have telegraphed my question loud and clear because Sal reached down and lifted the book from the shelf as tenderly as if she was picking up a newborn.

'This is the book my brother published just before his death,' Sal said softly, stroking the book with wrinkled hands. 'He was almost finished with his doctorate when ... well, when it happened. I was glad to have this to remember him by.'

I was beginning to think that the Bacon family might be something to contend with. After all, Sal's brother seemed to know how to manipulate folks and their minds, while Sal herself was someone you wouldn't want for an enemy. I figured that I'd need to rethink ol' Annie Bronson as well.

I returned to my browsing in Sal's private library. If we had to stay here much longer – not that I was complaining, mind – I needed something constructive to do.

Unlike Ellie, I liked to read things like books, not all that abstract nonsense like reading cards.

Behind me I could hear Ellie and Sal chatting, the rocking chair squeaking gently on the worn carpet. Calm had settled down over the room like an old familiar quilt, and I found I'd forgotten for a few minutes why we were even here. Chicken soup can do that to me.

I suddenly recalled some of Sal's earlier comments that had made me think she knew something about the fake ID ring. I replaced the book on the shelf and stood up, curious about how much she knew. With Detective Annie Bronson as her niece ... well, Aunt Sal was probably pretty savvy when it came to the local crime scene.

'Sal,' I ventured, verbally stepping all over Ellie in my curiosity, 'I'm wondering exactly how much you know about ... you know, about the problems at the Miramar.'

The rocking chair came to an abrupt halt. I could almost hear the protest from its rockers as Sal firmly planted both feet on the floor and looked me square in the eyes.

'I know about as much as you two, AJ.' Her canny expression spoke volumes, and I had a feeling that she was one up in the information department.

Ellie and I exchanged uneasy glances. We actually didn't know much, aside from the fact that three people were dead, there was a list of names that seemed to be important enough to kill for, and we were on the run for our lives. Other than that, we knew zilch.

I cleared my throat, more of a silence-filler than for any other reason. It's one of my nervous tics, kind of like chewing fingernails or picking at your cuticles. I needed to know exactly what Sal knew and if she had some ideas that would: a) save me and Ellie from certain death and; b) get us out of San Blanco and back on the road to home sweet home.

'OK,' I said, sounding like a cardsharp trying to bluff information from an opponent. 'This is what I know, what we know,' indicating Ellie with a nod. 'Three people are dead. Ellie recovered a list of names and one of the dead men was on the list. His brother has been arrested for harassing me and Ellie, and someone took potshots at us today.' I looked at her expectantly, waiting for her to show her hand.

Sal stared up at the ceiling, eyes narrowed in thought. She stayed that way for so long I was afraid she might have gone catatonic on us. As nervous as I was already, her sudden 'aha!' nearly stopped my heart.

'Annie told me about an identification theft ring she's been investigating for a while. She and that ex-whatever of hers, that Detective Fischer, found some links to the Miramar resort and they'd sent a few folks in to nose around.' Here Ellie and I looked at one another in surprise. Who in the world was she talking about? 'Unfortunately, you two came along and seemed to get in the middle of the whole thing.' I began to protest, but she shut me up with a majestic motion of her hand. How was I to know anything about what was going down at the Miramar? 'Annie rang me up and told me that you'd be at her house and to keep an eye out, which is what I was doing when you came tearing over that fence.'

Well, I suppose I should have been relieved that Sal Bacon didn't tote that gun around all the time. I didn't need another person gunning for me, pun clearly intended. Ellie stirred around, hands fiddling in her hair. I could tell she was itching to get to those cards; her own nervous tics give it away.

'If you two don't have any more questions, I need to start powering down for the evening.' She got to her feet, pausing to let her body adjust to the movement. Startled, Ellie and I glanced at each other. Sal sounded like she intended to dock the small house at some space station and recharge. Come to think about it, I wouldn't have been surprised in the least to see her take out a talkie-thingy like I saw in every space movie and say something like, 'Beam me up, Scotty.' San Blanco was fast becoming home of the weird and weirder.

'Is there anything I can do?' I figured if Sal was going to lock us all in for the night, it would be smart to know exactly how to reverse everything in order to spring myself and Ellie to safety.

'If you'd like, you can walk the perimeter with me,' answered Sal, pulling a tatty old cardigan from the closet by the front door. She gave me the once over then tossed an equally worn jacket my way. 'Better bundle up. It can get a tad nippy out there.'

Where were we headed? To the North Pole? As far as I knew, this was summer in a coastal town, and the chill really didn't set in until the sun went down.

'Should I go, too?' Ellie's voice sounded uncertain, and I could tell that she didn't relish the idea of being inside alone.

To my amusement, Sal opened the closet once more but instead of pulling out another sweater, she reached in and fished out another rifle. She tossed it to Ellie who caught it with one hand. The look on her face was hilarious, or at least it might have been if I hadn't known how petrified she was of anything that required ammunition.

'I'll stay, Ellie. You go with Sal,' I offered, taking off the jacket and holding out my hand for the gun.

'No, it's fine, AJ, really,' said Ellie with an offended look as if I'd just called her a sissy. Really. There's just no understanding her sometimes, you know?

'Let's go,' commanded Sal, striding to the door with her rifle over her shoulder. 'We'll be back in two shakes of a lamb's tail.'

As she walked through the door, I looked back over my shoulder and grinned at Ellie. I was starting to think we'd been transported into the Midwest somewhere and not to San Blanco's resort area.

Sal was moving at a fast clip, heading for the area by the rear of her house. By now, the sun had set sufficiently for the edges of the property to be thrown into shadow. I trotted to keep up with her, reminding myself that I really needed to start exercising. It's embarrassing when an old gal can out-walk you without all the huffing and puffing I was doing.

I could see an old shed, outlined in sunset, leaning into a stand of eucalyptus trees. That seemed to be our target, and when Sal pulled out a bunch of keys from the pocket of her pants and unlocked the door, I could clearly see why. Tucked into every corner and on every available surface were the accoutrements of a police officer's dream: large metal flashlights; packages of batteries; stacks of goggles both for night vision and the kind used at a shooting range; boxes of ammunition. It looked liked she'd robbed the local precinct.

'Here, take one of these.' Sal tossed a flashlight at me.

I caught it by mere chance, not being one of those talented folks who can snag a baseball out of the air with one hand without even looking. Call it a self-preservation move – the thing weighed at least three pounds and could have done some real damage.

'How do you keep this stuff out here,' I asked, looking around the shed, 'without anyone taking it?'

Sal barked a laugh. 'You're kidding, right? No one breaks into Sal Bacon's property. Not unless they want a wrasslin' match with a bear. And I say, if you're going to be a bear, be a grizzly.'

She grinned at me, turning around to leave the shed. I'm sure it was just a trick of the rapidly disappearing light, but I could have sworn I saw a row of teeth that any bear would have been proud to own. Shaking my head, I followed her out into the yard.

Chapter Twenty-six

By 'patrolling the perimeter', Sal meant just that. With me still slightly out of breath – the stop at the shed had let my lungs recover a bit – we marched around the edges of her property. The weather had turned chilly, so I was grateful for the jacket. Sal did her thing in complete silence, stopping every so often to poke her rifle into the undergrowth or to peer over the fence that surrounded most of the land. Who or what she was looking for I had no idea, but I figured I'd know it when she found it. Or them.

The flashlight I carried was indeed a lethal weight, and I amused myself by thinking of folks who deserved a rap over the noggin, beginning with David. I hadn't spared many thoughts for him lately, so I supposed I was on the road to recovery. For that matter, Detective Baird's dimpled face hadn't entered my mind either. Did that mean I was losing interest in men in general or just those two in particular? Hmm. That would be a challenge for Ellie and her ever-lovin' cards. I grinned to myself. Giving my cousin permission to dig into my private life was like tossing Hershey bars to a chocoholic.

Sal's steps halted abruptly and I almost knocked into her. I'd been so caught up in my own thoughts that I hadn't noticed what had gotten her attention. Putting a knotted finger to her mouth, Sal nodded in the direction of the back door to her house. It stood slightly open, a thin stream of light creeping around the door frame. I frowned. We'd gone out the front door, locking it securely behind us, and I couldn't remember if the back had been left open or not. By the way Sal was reacting, though, my guess was for 'not'.

The silence in the house scared me more than if Ellie had been screaming her head off. Sal began inching toward the steps that led to the door, using the rifle to nudge it open. A sharp creak made me jump and I fully expected gunfire to erupt at any moment. There was nothing, though, nothing but the quiet of a house that is standing empty.

And that meant no Ellie.

Only, once we got inside, I could see that this wasn't the case at all. Ellie sat in the couch, not curled up and relaxed as she had been earlier, but ramrod straight, hands in lap and eyes opened as wide as they would go. Standing behind her and seated next to her were two of the toughest-looking men I'd ever had the misfortune of seeing. The one on the couch had both beefy arms crossed in front of him, one large tree trunk of a leg crossed over the other. His eyes, a deep blue and set too close to his nose for my taste, tracked Sal and me as we moved into the front room. I tried not to look directly at either guy; I've always heard stories about looking crazed animals in the eyes and then being attacked. I certainly didn't want *that* to happen, not to me, or Sal, or Ellie.

Sal stood frozen, rifle slung over her shoulder and one hand on her hip. She looked for all money like she'd just come from a day of hunting in the back forty, and the two visitors must've had the same idea. Instead of telling her to drop the gun, they simply raised theirs in a macabre greeting. I almost expected them to go into some hunt-inspired fist bump or something equally cheesy.

Ellie's frightened eyes met mine and I saw the tiniest tremble on her lips. My blood started to boil. I have these family defense genes that kick into high gear whenever someone in my clan is being harassed or hurt, and Ellie was clan. I slid my eyes around the room as cautiously as possible, not wanting to attract unnecessary attention. I needed a starting point for my campaign, somewhere to aim for when I made my first move.

Unfortunately for me, this first move included handing over my flashlight to Goon Number Two who moved from behind the couch and wordlessly held out his hand. I've never claimed to be brave, just defensive. Without a sound, he pocketed my would-be weapon in his jacket pocket and resumed his post behind Ellie.

'McClellan. What a surprise.' Sal's words were dry as unbuttered toast, and I saw the man on the couch eye her with undisguised hatred. Well. Sal obviously hadn't made a friend here, and I was beginning to get an idea of where she'd met him before.

'We don't need none of your guff, Bacon,' retorted Keith McClellan, for that's indeed who it was: another name from the list.

'That's *Detective* Bacon to you,' Sal replied calmly, turning her gaze to Ellie.

'You OK, sweetie?'

Ellie glanced nervously at her two captors, obviously too scared to speak for herself. The man who'd pocketed the flashlight clapped one large hand on her shoulder and answered for her.

'She's fine. In fact, she insisted we wait for you two so's we could get this here little party started.' His thin smile didn't quite make the journey all the way to his cold dark eyes. By process of elimination, I'd figured that I was looking at the first name on the list, José Ramirez Something-or-other.

'And Rascon, too. How can a gal get so lucky,' Sal drawled, all but rolling her eyes. She remained on her feet, and I noticed McClellan's eyes had shifted to the rifle held loosely in her hands. Before I could get another thought pieced together, he sprang from the couch and lunged at

Sal. I screamed. I shouldn't have worried, though. With one swift step to the side and a chop to the bridge of his nose with the rifle butt, it was suddenly three to one, advantage Team Bacon.

Ellie, moving with more alacrity than I'd seen since we were kids running from Sammy Burkheart and his pump-action air rifle filled with rock salt, leapt to her feet and all but flew at me. I grabbed her and together we raced out the back door, leaving Sal to tackle Rascon alone. Oddly enough, I wasn't worried.

'We've gotta get some help.' Ellie's teeth were chattering so much I almost couldn't understand her. Shock was setting in rapidly and I knew from experience that if I didn't get something into her soon – of course, I was thinking sugar – she'd be unable to move on her own accord.

I chewed my lip, trying to come up with a plan that would make sense. My first instinct, naturally, was to run screaming for help, but all that would do for us was put a target on our backs. And if my calculations were right, there was still one name on the list that was unaccounted for: Richard Olsen. For all I knew, he was standing guard somewhere nearby, waiting for his *compadres* to get rid of three more witnesses. That thought scared me into action.

Taking Ellie's arm, I all but dragged her back toward the little shed. I hoped with all my heart that Sal had forgotten to lock it, although I sincerely doubted that would be the case. Anyone as security savvy as Sal wouldn't forget a detail as important as that.

Someone must have been watching out for us. To my surprise, the lock gave way easily, its hasp not fully secured by the heavy bolt. Thanking my lucky stars and vowing to start giving more thought to churchgoing once more, which would thrill my mother no end, I dragged Ellie inside. The sun had disappeared completely now and the shed was in total darkness. I felt my way around the small room, trying to remember exactly where the flashlights had been stored. I didn't need a light as much as I needed something heavy to knock some would-be killer over the head.

I could still hear Ellie's teeth chattering against one another. She was in serious condition, no big surprise there, considering all she'd been through in the past few days. Chancing Olsen's location, I crouched down and switched the light on, holding the bulb end close to the floor. Ellie stood where I'd left her, her eyes focused on something I couldn't see. She looked awful.

'Ellie, I want you to stay in here. I'm going to get some help, OK?' I rose to my feet, grasping both her arms in mine, forcing her to look at me. 'OK, Ellie?'

She nodded slowly, but I could see that some of the color was coming back into her face. I was relieved; it looked like she'd be fine to leave for a while. I didn't have much time, though, and I knew it. It would only be a matter of minutes before someone, either Olsen or Rascon, would be out looking for us.

I grabbed another flashlight and handed it her before heading back out into the darkness. I've never been overly excited about ghost hunts, or haunted houses, or anything that makes me jump, so it was no surprise that my heart had begun to pick up speed with my first tentative steps. I held my breath, forcing the rhythm to slow down. I might need to run and having a pulse already at sky-high levels would probably not be a good thing.

I looked around the yard, waiting for my eyes to fully adjust themselves to the blackness. It took just a few seconds, but it felt like an eternity. All I needed now was for someone to come pouncing out of the night and take me down. Ellie would be trapped in the shed and Sal would be left to fend for herself against the marauders. I shivered, and it wasn't from the cold. I still had that old ratty jacket on, glad now that I'd taken it from Sal.

Slipping my hands into the pockets, I froze: something cold and metallic and cellphone size met my fingers. There was no way, I thought stupidly. I'd seen Sal's cellphone and it was in *her* pocket. How in the Sam Hill had it managed to find its way to my jacket?

Whirling around, I ran back toward the shed. I needed to get to Ellie and call the San Blanco PD. I was two steps away, no more, when a voice reached my ears.

'Well, well, now. If it isn't Little Miss Nosey herself. I thought I told you to get lost. Too bad you don't take friendly advice.' The words were spoken in a low tone, so soft that if I had wanted to, I could have convinced myself that I'd imagined the whole thing. Unfortunately, I don't have that good an imagination.

The man who stepped forward from the shadows was tall, that much I could tell. If his voice was anything to judge, he was also dangerous. I'd seen movies where the hit man or assassin or mob don would speak softly, almost kindly, just before he let go with a blast from his gun.

OK – maybe I *did* have an imagination. What I wouldn't have given at that moment to be wrong. Or at least to have seen different movies. Knowledge may be power, but it's also painful, especially when you know what's coming. Taking a deep breath, I turned toward the voice.

And froze in astonishment. I realized that I had known Richard Olsen all along.

Chapter Twenty-seven

Have you ever had one of the moments, an epiphany of sorts, when it dawns on you that you've played right into the hands of the enemy? Well, that was my moment, standing in the chill San Blanco evening, fingers curled around a lifeline – my cellphone – and staring danger straight in the eyes …

Detective Baird, dimple and all, faced me across the yard. I felt like my feet were nailed to the ground as he sauntered over to me, one hand resting lightly on the nine millimeter handgun strapped to his side. I felt confused, betrayed. Did police officers really 'go bad' as they did in the cop shows I watched? (Note to self: change viewing habits immediately!) Maybe he was here to help. Or maybe he was here to …

I heard the tiniest of creaks behind me. Ellie, or someone, was trying to open the shed door as softly as possible. I truly hoped that it was Ellie and not one of the thugs from the house. I thought quickly, trying to formulate a plan. If we could trade places, if I could get Baird (I couldn't bring myself to add the moniker 'Detective' to his name) to move somehow, so that his back was to the shed, we might have a chance. I wasn't quite sure what the chance might consist of, but I was desperate.

With my heart thudding somewhere in my throat, I stepped forward.

'So. Nice to see you – I don't think,' I added sarcastically. I could see a grin spread across his face.

Good to know I could still entertain.

I took another step toward him then casually, as if I had no other thought than to get a better look at him, I turned around with my back toward the house. He stayed put, though, not taking the bait.

Move, you big jerk, I screamed silently, willing him to turn his back to the shed. He did, to my great astonishment. I'd have to remember to tell Ellie that I possibly had some sixth sense-type abilities as well. If I managed to get out of this alive, of course.

We stood staring at one another, an 'OK Corral' stand-off in Sal Bacon's backyard. I hoped it would end with me still standing and him in handcuffs, though. I didn't want to think about what the other possibility could be. I fished around in my mind for something to say, something that would at least stall the inevitable, but my thoughts wouldn't slow down long enough for me to catch one. Instead, I did what came most naturally to me: I opened my mouth and let 'er fly.

'How'd you find me?' Stupid, really stupid. Of course he knew exactly how to find me, since he was the one who'd suggested Annie Bronson's house in the first place, and had probably already known that this was where we were, assuming that he'd spoken to Annie. And there was no reason why he wouldn't talk to her. They were on the same team, after all, or at least that's what Annie would expect, and she wouldn't think twice about sharing information with a fellow detective.

As I stood looking at the man I'd once thought to be the most handsome person I'd ever set eyes on, I could feel my blood pressure starting to rise. What *was* it with men? The best-looking ones were absolute failures as potential partners, and even a uniform wasn't a complete guarantee. I gritted my teeth. I was either going to burst a blood vessel or tell this jerk what I really thought.

'You are the most inane, scummy, low-down excuse

for a man that I have ever met, you know that, *Detective* Baird?' I made the word sound like a slur, and from the way his jaw line tightened, he'd gotten my message, no question. That might not have been the wisest thing to do at that moment, but I was furious. I'd been outsmarted, tricked, by a dimple. How dumb can you get, AJ?

He took a step toward me, and I involuntarily moved back. I wasn't scared any more, or at least not to the degree I had been at first, but I still had no desire to tangle with someone almost twice my size and probably ten times my strength. Better to keep some space between us.

Over his shoulder I saw movement. Purposely keeping my eyes firmly on his, I moved another few paces backward. I could see that his mind was moving, trying to figure out just what I was up to. If I could keep him focused on me just one more minute or so ...

With a yell that seemed to come from her belly, my cousin, the crazy, card-reading, sometimes irritating Ellie Saddler, burst out of the shed, a metal flashlight raised above her head like a club. Whenever I think about this scene, it always seems to play out in slow motion: Ellie racing toward Baird; Baird's face a mixture of anger and surprise as he turns to face her; me leaping forward to knock him off balance. Her weapon caught him on the side of the head, causing him to stagger but not go down.

Ellie, possessed by something unworldly – I swear I'd never seen her act this crazed before – continued to bring the heavy flashlight down on Baird, making contact wherever she could.

Baird sank to his knees then slowly, very slowly, toppled onto his side. Blood was streaming down his face and out of the various cuts she had opened on his scalp, and he lay absolutely still. I reached over him to grab Ellie's hand. She was poised to take another shot at him, but I figured if she kept on like this, she'd kill the jerk. And I wanted nothing more than to see his worthless hide go to prison.

'Ellie, it's all right, it's all right. You got him,' I said softly to her, working the flashlight from her grasp. 'It's OK.'

She looked at me then, her eyes filled with tears. 'Did I kill him, AJ?'

I wanted to laugh. Soft-hearted Ellie, always worried about the other person. 'Naw. Too bad, though. If anyone deserves it, he does, that's for sure.'

A groan came from the figure lying at our feet. I looked down at Baird, wanting to give him a swift kick where it would really hurt. First things first, though.

'Ellie, give me your belt.' I was unbuckling my own and pulling it off while I spoke. 'Let's get this animal's feet and hands tied up nice and tight.'

We set to work disabling Baird. I gave my belt an extra hard tug when I fastened it around his wrists, making sure that the sharp-edged buckle was pressing into his back. Ellie's belt, a fashionable linen number, was used to anchor his ankles together. He had lapsed into unconsciousness again, and I gave him a none-too-gentle tap on the top of the head just to make sure he'd stay that way. We didn't need him getting mobile before the real officers got here.

The back door to Sal's house banged open. Ellie and I looked up to see Sal standing there. Unfortunately, someone else was also there, a shiny silver gun pressed to the side of Sal's head. José Ramirez Rascon, his ugly mug set in a scowl, now had a hostage. And we had a huge problem.

'Untie him. Now,' Rascon commanded.

I didn't move, couldn't move, more from fright than stubbornness. Ellie, on the other hand, had not just regained her composure, she was channeling that same crazy recklessness that had fueled her attack on Baird. I watched in amazement as my cousin, always so careful to preserve her own skin, sauntered toward Rascon and Sal, one hand on her hip and the other casually swinging the flashlight like a baton. I groaned. I could not watch my best friend mown down in her prime right before my eyes. I squeezed them shut, praying for a miracle but hearing instead the unmistakable sound of a gun being fired.

With my ears reverberating from the blast, I kept my eyes shut tight for another few seconds, not wanting to see the inevitable. When I opened them again, I could have fallen over. Ellie had not only walked straight up to Rascon, she'd coolly swung the flashlight smack against his jaw, almost cold-cocking the man. Sal, acting on instinct, threw an elbow into his rather ponderous gut just as she ducked under the gun's muzzle, causing his shot to go wide.

My guess was that Rascon, self-professed tough guy, could handle bossing other men around but had no idea how to handle a woman who had not only disobeyed a direct order, but also made a monkey out of his machismo. He all but invited Ellie to whack him a good one by letting her get that close to him, so it was really his own fault. Men.

Who can figure?

Sal got to her feet, moving a bit slowly, but with a look of triumph on her face like she'd just won the Lottery. She brushed her hands off, rubbing them against her pants, before turning to check on Ellie.

Ellie stood on the bottom step, looking down at the huddled form of José Ramirez Rascon. He was out cold. Sal reached over and grabbed at the gun, making sure to unload the ammunition before jamming it into her pocket. I just stood there, unsure what I needed to do. It was one of those weird moments when time seems to be moving much faster than you are and it feels like your feet haven't quite got the hang of walking in tandem.

The night air was definitely cooler now, so I stuck my

hands in my pockets and encountered the cellphone again. Pulling it out, I flipped it open and stared at it. I felt numb, so much had happened in one short hour. Who should I call? For that matter, who in the world would believe what I'd seen? Without really thinking about it, I began dialing Detective Fischer's number from memory.

'Fischer,' he answered, sounding like I'd caught him in the middle of a meal. In between listening to the chewing on the other end of the line, I managed to get across what had happened. When I'd finally said all I had to say, there was complete silence on the other end.

'Detective? We really need someone out here pronto. We've got all three suspects down, two out and one coming around.' I could hear moans generating from inside the open door, and I wanted back-up from the law before any of the three were able to get ambulatory again.

'Already done. In fact,' here he paused and swallowed again, 'if you look just to the east of Sal's gate, you should see my car.'

Sure enough, the faint gleam from the foglights on the patrol car could be seen, and when he turned on the headlights, I could see that he was followed by two other cruisers. The cavalry had arrived.

It turned out that Sal Bacon had a nosey neighbor, Old Man Southeby, whose property butted up to Sal's land just behind the line of eucalyptus trees. When Baird had shown up, hiding his traitorous self among the trees, Southeby had seen movement and was just curious enough to sneak out in time to listen to our exchange. He'd called the San Blanco PD while Ellie and I were tying Baird up. Help had already been on the way when Ellie had played hero.

The three of us, Ellie, Sal, and I, stood in the front yard, watching as each police car hauled off a perp. Baird, his head bloody and still a tad woozy from Ellie's talent with the flashlight, was taken away by a young officer. When Baird was marched past Fischer, the evening's most telling moment occurred. Fischer, moving slowly and deliberately, spit a wad of gum on the ground (at least that's what it looked like from where I was standing) and turned his back on his former partner. Baird's humiliation was complete.

Chapter Twenty-eight

Although the entire ID theft ring gang was either dead or locked up and couldn't hurt anyone else, I still felt antsy and wanted to get the heck out of Dodge; after all, a killer *was* still stalking the resort. Ellie had found a place to rest at Sal Bacon's house and she was in no hurry to get back to the humdrum of our little hometown.

'I mean, really, AJ,' she said the next day as she lay on the hammock that Sal had strung between two eucalyptus trees, 'how can you top this?' Sipping her iced tea and looking at me innocently, I could have gladly popped her a good one. But since she'd saved my life, and Sal's, too, for that matter, I left her alone to enjoy the sun.

I wandered through the backyard, stopping to examine the spot where my heart had been destroyed yet again, left in a puddle of blood. Not literally, of course, but figuratively; when Baird had betrayed the department, he had also betrayed me. I shook my head sadly, wondering what it was about me that seemed to find and fall for these cretins so effortlessly.

'AJ! You're wanted on the phone,' Sal called from the open kitchen window which overlooked the backyard.

I lifted a hand to her in acknowledgement, giving one last look at the ground.

Time to move on, I thought. Chin up, AJ.

I stepped through the kitchen door, my eyes still dazzled from the bright sunshine.

Sal nodded toward an old-fashioned phone that sat on a small table in one corner of the kitchen. I almost laughed when I saw it. Compared to her hi-tech satellite contraption, this was a complete dinosaur.

'This is AJ.' I spoke into the phone's plastic mouthpiece, watching Sal as she puttered around the kitchen, humming tunelessly and getting lunch ready. Ellie and I would be completely spoiled if we stayed here much longer.

'AJ, Stan West here. How are you?' The clipped tones of the Miramar's general manager came over the line, sounding cordial and businesslike. I'd heard him use just this very manner when trying to manipulate folks into doing what he wanted, so I was wary, instantly on my guard. I mean, why in the world would he be calling just to ask me how I was?

'I'm well, thanks. How's it going at the Miramar?' What a Class 'A' dummy. I'd just given him the perfect segue for what he really wanted.

'Amazingly enough, that's why I'm calling you,' Stan cleared his throat uneasily.

Here it comes, I thought ruefully. I'd walked right into his trap.

'Is there a chance that you could come back to the Miramar and give me a hand? Just for a few days,' he added hastily.

I was silent, turning his request over in my head. I wasn't sure if Ellie would want to go back there, and I sure wasn't going back by myself.

'AJ? Are you still there?' To his credit, Stan didn't sound too sure of himself, something that I detest. If someone gets pushy with me, I tend to cut them off.

'Yes, I am. Can I get back to you? I'll need to check on my cousin's plans before I make a commitment one way or the other.' There. It wasn't an outright 'no', so it should keep him happy for a while, at least until I talked to Ellie.

'Absolutely, AJ. No problem. And tell your cousin ... Ellie, is it? She's welcome here as well. Same benefits as you get.' Stan was clearly relieved and rang off quickly before I could change my mind and turn him down.

Fabulous. Talk about coming full circle: if I wasn't careful, I'd end up back in the thick of things again. I knew enough from speaking to Annie, and listening to the other officers' conversations, that this ID theft ring affair wasn't over. The Miramar was still the focus of an active investigation, and if there was someone out there who'd just as soon kill you as smile at you, I did not want to meet him, free cookies or not.

'What do you need to talk to me about?'

Ellie had come into the kitchen so quietly that it hadn't registered, and I nearly dropped the phone when she spoke.

'Good grief, Ellie! Do you really need to sneak up on me like that?' I sounded irritated because I was. I was mad at myself for falling into the Miramar snare again, and I was irked at being caught out by Ellie before formulating a plan. Now I'd have to think on my feet, something I wasn't too good at.

'Well, aren't we just the little Miss Mary Sunshine,' said Ellie, said, snagging a hot roll from the plate on the kitchen table. She took a bite, eyes closed with exaggerated pleasure. 'These are awesome, Sal! You're rapidly becoming my most favorite cook ever.'

She stuck her tongue out at me, crumbs and all. Just like when we were kids, trying to butter up – pun clearly intended here – Grandma Tillie. I returned the gesture. Sometimes we acted like we were ten and not two grown women.

'Well?' She paused by the table, popping the last piece of roll into her mouth. 'What was it you need to talk to me about?'

'Nothing. Well, something, but nothing important. Sal, can I help you with anything?' I deliberately cut Ellie's questioning short. I was still smart enough to choose my own place and time to discuss something like going back to the Miramar.

'AJ,' Ellie said in a warning tone. 'You might as well tell me. I'm just going to hassle you until you give it up, AJ.'

And she wasn't kidding. Ellie Saddler could worry information out of someone faster than a dog could get to a bone's marrow. It's a talent that I've always wished fervently I had. When it came to the manipulating gene in the Saddler DNA, Ellie had clearly gotten the lion's share.

'Oh, all right,' I said, giving in without a fight. If I didn't tell her now, she'd drive me crazy until I did. 'Stan West, the Miramar's manager, wants me, wants us, to come back. That's all.' I casually got my own roll from the steaming pile and bit into it. Better to let Ellie turn the information over in her head than to offer an opinion.

I didn't have long to wait for a response.

'He *what?*' Ellie's voice rose, her color following suit. 'I can't believe it! The *nerve* of that man! After the way he treated us? Well, he's got another think coming if he thinks …' She broke off her tirade as Sal, wiping her hands on a towel, calmly turned around from the stove.

'Have you considered the possibility of going back, AJ?' Her eyes found Ellie. 'I know you had a lot of upsetting things happen there at the resort, but with the case still open, well, I'm sure that you would be of great help to Annie.' She smiled at us, innocence on her face and in her voice. I wasn't buying it for a minute.

'Sal, I'm not sure if you actually know what happened to us there,' I protested. 'I mean, what with Ellie practically being killed in our own room and all those bodies, I'm not too crazy about getting back there any time soon.'

Ellie nodded her head in agreement. 'Sal, there is way too much going on at that place. If Annie could guarantee that we'd be safe, I might consider it, but not until then. No way.' She looked at me for confirmation and I nodded back. At least we could agree on one thing.

Now *that* was an interesting idea, I mused. If Annie was to give us some kind of protection, maybe invent another cousin who 'happened' to be hanging around in San Blanco in general and the Miramar in particular, I might consider it, 'might' being the operative word.

Sal's sixth sense, the thing that had made her a bloodhound as a detective, must have felt my hesitation. She added, in a reasonable-sounding voice, 'You know, Annie might just consider that. Especially if it meant that the case could be wrapped up.'

Great. Now my guilt was being played like a harp. My mother, bless her heart, had managed to hone that part of my psyche through looks of disappointment and deep sighs whenever I misbehaved, acting as though I had just crushed her life's dream. All I needed now was a surrogate mother to push me into doing something I didn't really want to do. Needed it like a hole in the head.

'Fine,' I heard myself saying ungraciously. 'Let me call Stan back.' Ellie's look of amusement didn't help my mood much either; I hated feeling like I had been tricked. 'And I'll let him know that the TWO of us will be there tomorrow.' There. That would fix Ellie's wagon, I thought smugly. If I had to do this, then she did, too.

Sal's smile was like the sun. 'I'll give Annie a call right now. You girls are doing a good thing. I mean it.' With that, she left the kitchen, heading to her office, presumably to use her satellite phone. That, or she didn't want us to hear what she was going to say. There was no telling what she and Annie would cook up between the two of them.

I could feel Ellie staring at me. I took the high road. I also got in the first comment.

'Well, you know how I get, Ellie,' I said plaintively. 'If someone needs something, I just can't say no.'

Ellie snorted. 'No joke. Isn't that how you got involved with David?'

Score one for Ellie. She knew just how low to hit. My next move had to be conciliatory or I'd never hear the end of this.

'Ellie, I really need you there with me.' Good grief AJ, I scolded myself. You sound like a baby who can't go into a dark room by herself.

It worked. Ellie's ego is a tad larger than the norm, and she loves to be stroked and petted, told how much everyone else depends on her. She smiled at me magnanimously.

'Of course you need me, AJ. It's a good thing I'd already decided to do it.'

Now it was my turn to grunt derisively. 'Whatever. Maybe if you could read your cards, we'd know what to expect.'

And with that dig, I walked back outside, breathing in the salt-laden breeze. I knew that I'd eventually have to go back home, but until then I'd suck it up. San Blanco had been good for a change, even if it had given me a few potholes along the way.

Ellie followed me but I ignored her, strolling out into the yard and toward the front of the house. I stopped near the end of the rutted driveway, staring across the field toward Annie's house. If we could just get back in …

Ellie came up behind me. I could hear her soft breathing as she stood silently and I knew that she was either looking for a fight or a way to make up.

'I need to go over to Annie's,' she announced, her voice close to my ear. I turned around to look at her, catching the tail end of a smile on her lips. Good – the fight had been shelved, at least for the time being. Knowing Ellie and myself, though, we'd get back to it eventually.

'I was just thinking that myself,' I admitted, turning

back to look at the house. 'There has to be some way to … hey, I wonder if Sal has a spare key? She could go with us, pull guard duty with that gun of hers, while we collect our things. What do you think?'

Ellie nodded thoughtfully. 'That sounds like a better plan than I had. I figured we could just go back over the wall and jimmy the door or a window.'

I laughed; sometimes she can be so silly. The funny thing is, I think she was serious.

'Let's go talk to Sal. She probably has lunch ready for us anyways. Last one to the table is a rotten egg!'

I took off running before I'd finished talking, which was absolutely not fair but hey! That's the way it goes in families sometimes.

Chapter Twenty-nine

Sal insisted on driving us over to Annie's even though we could see it from the front yard.

'We still have to haul all your things back, girls, and I'm not a pack mule.' She didn't take the rifle as I'd assumed she would, instead slipping a cute little .22 pistol into the ankle holster she'd retrieved from her store room. I grinned, wondering what my mother would say if she knew I was consorting with old ladies who preferred a good firearm to a man.

The house looked like a whirlwind had gone through it. Couch cushions and pillows lay strewn across the front-room floor, and Annie's collection of old police manuals had been dumped from the bookshelf where she had lined them up in precise order. I bent to gather some of the books but Sal stopped me with a quick word.

'I know they already got pictures in here, AJ, but Annie said to leave it all the way we found it. She's funny that way about her things.' Sal disappeared into the kitchen and I could hear the sound of water being run. I guess 'don't touch' didn't extend to relatives who raised you.

Ellie and I made quick work of getting our gear together and lugging it back out to the car. Ellie had tucked her cards into her pocket, placing all her other belongings in her overnight bag. As for my things, I had shoved them into the suitcase willy-nilly, wanting nothing more than to get out of the house and back to Sal's. The atmosphere still held an aura of violence and I had the uncomfortable feeling that if we were to linger much longer, we might be run out again at the point of a gun. Silly, I know, but there it was: I was completely creeped out. And if Detective Annie Bronson's bungalow made me feel this way, how in the world would I be able to function at the Miramar?

Sal definitely made the visit to Annie's easier. I wished that she could go with us, but I figured that it would need to be someone younger and probably a member of the San Blanco PD.

Wait – Sal had been a police officer! And she still had a mean hand when it came to firearms and police procedures and the like. Why couldn't *she* go with us? Maybe pose as our Grandma Tillie? I was pretty pleased with my own suggestion, and Ellie caught me in mid-grin.

'What's so funny, AJ?' she demanded, folding her arms and giving me her famous 'it had better not be me making you laugh' stare.

'Your face,' I retorted childishly, then softened the comment with a jab at her arm.

When we were younger, Ellie and I had started fake-punching one another, something that drove our mothers crazy. They had done their best to turn us into proper young ladies, and they would say whenever they caught us exchanging blows, 'A lady never resorts to violence.' For some perverse reason, that would make us giggle. As we grew older, it ceased to be so amusing but we still hung onto the detestable – in our mothers' eyes – habit of punching each other's arms.

'Now, now, girls,' chided Sal as we pulled into the bumpy driveway. She pulled the behemoth of a vehicle back into its familiar spot and cut the engine. 'Don't you two ever get along for more than a few minutes?' Shaking her head in mock exasperation, she opened the heavy car door and stepped out into the yard.

I waited until we were all seated at the kitchen table to bring up the idea of Sal going undercover with us to the

Miramar. Ellie had her beloved cards spread out in front of her. She had started making the pattern that I had seen before, occasionally flipping a card over and setting it aside. I watched her face rather than her hands, looking for a clue as to what she was thinking. The cards I didn't trust, but Ellie's instincts I did.

Sal brought a pitcher of iced tea over along with three old-fashioned jelly-jar glasses. I hadn't seen anything like that since the time Ellie and I had to stay with Great-Aunt Augusta while our folks went to a funeral. I tell you – that woman made me feel nervous, even as a little girl. Sometimes I had a hard time believing she was my beloved Grandma Tillie's sister.

'Sal,' I began, reaching over to help myself to a glass of tea. 'I have a proposition for you.' I took the first taste of the cool amber-colored liquid, letting it slide down my throat slowly. There's just nothing better than iced tea – unsweetened, of course – on a warm day.

'Fire away.' Sal looked evenly at me across the table, sipping at her own glass. I didn't know her well enough to read her face, but she probably could keep her reactions under wraps from her days behind the badge.

'I think it would be awesome if you'd come with me and Ellie back to the Miramar, Sal. Now hang on a sec,' I said firmly, holding up one hand as Sal started to speak. 'You're an officer, you know how to handle a gun, and you could be our Grandma Tillie, come down for a bit of sun.'

Ellie looked up from her cards, a troubled look on her face. 'AJ, I don't think that's such a good idea. I just saw something that worries me about this whole going-back thing.'

Sal and I both turned to face Ellie. She really did sound concerned, and like I said before, I do trust her instincts. Still …

'What do you think is going to happen, Ellie?' Sal beat

me to the punch. I'd seen her eying the cards as Ellie had laid them out, a look of curiosity on her face.

Ellie sat silently, looking down at the two cards she had turned over. When she looked up, I swore I could see real fear in her eyes.

'I can only tell you what the cards are saying,' she answered slowly. She picked up one of the cards, fingers trembling. 'This is The High Priestess. This means that we need to follow woman's intuition. But it's upside down, so it means we can't rely on our instincts.'

'OK, no prob,' I replied, trying to lighten the moment. 'I guess we'll just have to solve this little issue with our smarts.'

'What does this one mean?' Sal pointed to a card with a man hanging from a tree.

'That is The Hanging Man, and it means that we are almost guaranteed to fail in whatever we try to do.' Ellie sounded depressed, and I impulsively reached over and squeezed her arm. She can be a real worry-wart at times.

Sal was beginning to look serious. I could almost see the smoke coming out of her ears as she thought things over, weighing the options against Ellie's words. To tell the truth, that surprised me. For some reason I assumed that officers used deductive reasoning and not tarot cards to figure out the next move. This whole business of card reading was getting on my nerves, though, and being the diplomatic woman that I am, I let Ellie know just how I felt.

'Look, Ellie,' I spoke up firmly. 'There is no way in the world I'm going to let a two by three piece of cardstock tell me what to think and feel and believe. We will either be successful or not at the Miramar, and that has nothing to do with fate or karma or whatever you want to call it.'

I was getting up a good head of steam, and from the looks of things, Ellie was as well. I'd already stepped in it almost up to my hips, so a few more words wouldn't make a difference.

'Sal, you know how to handle a situation, so you'd be perfect for going to the resort with us. Ellie, you can keep your eyes and ears open for any problems. I can make sure that none of us is left alone for any reason.' I paused to smile at Sal and Ellie.

'Look, we can do this, cards or no cards. Annie needs a break and Fischer deserves one, that's for sure. What the man must be going through right now!' I stopped talking to catch my breath, giving Ellie the perfect opportunity to barge in.

'AJ, you are an absolute dork. Don't you think that everyone will recognize Sal? I mean, she's been around here for ever, and they would already know that Annie is related to her.'

Ellie had jumped into the fray with both feet; it's too bad that one of them was needed for her 'open mouth, insert foot' problem.

'I will have you know, young lady, that I have *not* been around here "for ever", as you so succinctly put it.' Sal's hands were on her hips, her mouth folded as rigidly as one of Grandma Tillie's precious lace-trimmed linen tablecloths. She looked like a pint-sized version of those nutty wrestlers on local television. Ellie, her own mouth set in annoyance, looked ready to fire the next verbal salvo.

'Er ... Ellie, Sal, let's focus, OK?' I attempted to defuse the tense sparring match before it got much life, not wanting to alienate either woman. We needed to be a team if anything successful was going to come of this insane return to the Miramar. 'Sal, I think that you could use a little help in the disguise department. Ellie, could you help me think of something that could change her appearance? I mean, think Grandma Tillie here.'

Sometimes I just crack myself up, and I nearly got the giggles visualizing Sal as our grandmother. Our Grandma

Tillie is a mountain of a woman, and I do mean that in the nicest way. She is nearly as wide as she is tall, and she has the ability to move her heft as quickly as if she was half the size. It wasn't wise to tangle with Grandma Tillie; sassy little girls were never able to outrun the fly swatter of justice at her house.

I could see that Ellie was reading my mind as she smiled at me. Turning back to look at Sal, she said, 'Yes, I can see we'd need to add a few things, maybe some padding around the middle. Hey, AJ, you know that show we like to watch, the one where they explain how they do makeup for movies? They always stuff something in the person's mouth to, you know, to plump up their face.'

Ellie can use her words sometimes to get a point across in an oh-so-innocent way. I hastily added, 'Yes, they use something in the *cheeks* to make someone look heavier.'

I shot Ellie a warning glance. It wouldn't do to get Sal all riled up again.

Sal still looked doubtful. 'I'm not sure, girls. I need to talk to Annie first, run the whole scheme by her.'

'Great idea, Sal!' I said enthusiastically. 'Why don't you ring her right now?' No time like the present, I thought wryly, to tackle a bad idea.

In record time, the three of us were packed and ready to hit the trail for the Miramar. I called ahead to let Stan know that our 'grandma' would be joining us so he wouldn't pop a blood vessel when he saw an extra face at the table.

Whether I liked it or not, I was back in the saddle, heading right back into the mess I'd managed to escape. Who says dumb isn't contagious?

Chapter Thirty

From the outside, the Miramar Resort looked as placid as ever. The grounds were well-tended, the bougainvillea abounded with riotous fuchsia-colored blossoms, and the large windows of the main lobby gleamed in the sunlight. To the casual observer, this was a place of rest and relaxation, not the terrifying location I knew it to be. Just one more reason I was glad to have the comforting figure of Sal beside me.

The front desk clerk was happy to see me and Ellie again and only gave Sal a fleeting glance. So far, so good, on the covert end of things, although with the way Sal was conspicuously checking out the exits, I had the feeling that the undercover part might not last all that long.

I got the keycard to the Palo Verde suite again, though what possessed me to agree to that particular set of rooms is beyond me. It was probably more habit than anything else, but I could tell it didn't sit well with Ellie. Sal, on the other hand, was pleased, especially when she found out that this was the place we'd experienced some horrifying moments.

'I'm not a ghoul, girls,' she told us, 'just an old cop taking advantage of a crime scene.'

Whatever the reason, the Palo Verde it was. I was relieved to see that the place had been restored to pristine condition, no evidence of our run-in with the Ellie's assailant or the San Blanco PD's forensic team. All traces of black fingerprint powder were gone and the place looked fabulous.

I toted our luggage into the bedroom, then paused: I hadn't considered the sleeping arrangements and with just one bed and couch, one of the three of us might found our self on the floor. I shouldn't have bothered worrying, though. When I returned to the front room, Sal was already plumping and fluffing the couch cushions. She looked up as I walked in.

'Should be just fine out here. You two take the bedroom. I've got ol' Bessie here for company,' she added, lovingly patting her rifle.

I just shook my head. Ol' Bessie, and a couple of her smaller relatives, had made the trip in a battered golf bag that had definitely seen better *decades*, never mind days.

Well, if Sal felt safe, then I felt safe.

Ellie was sitting at the kitchen table, a brooding look on her face. I knew something was wrong, could probably even guess what it was, but I knew she'd tell me sooner or later. The ever-present deck of cards lay at her elbow, and I was pretty sure that before long, she'd have them spread out, poring over them and giving herself another ulcer.

'I guess I need to find what's-his-name, let him know we're here. Ellie,' I asked, looking at my cousin, 'do you want to go with me, or stay here with Sal?'

Ellie's hands moved over the cards, automatically picking them up and shuffling them as she thought.

'I think I'll stay, AJ. Sal and I can meet you for dinner, if you want to eat with everyone else. I mean, if we don't want room service.' She spoke almost absently as she began to lay the cards out on the table, moving them into precise rows that fanned out from a center card.

I shrugged. 'Sounds good. Talking to more than two people at one time might be too much for Stan anyway.' I'd never been overly impressed by his mental prowess; I'd seen him in action and he had been found wanting, in my opinion. Sigh. Never send a man to do a woman's work …

With the promise to call if I was held up for any reason, i.e. if Stan managed to dump his work on me, I left the suite and headed for the front lobby. The corridors were quiet, with none of the everyday sounds one might expect to hear at a hotel. Either it was an across-the-board siesta, or Stan had everyone cowed into silence.

As I passed the office where I'd been nearly frightened to death, I paused. There was no light shining under the door that I could see, but my ears had caught a sound, something almost metallic softly clicking inside.

Common sense would usually tell someone to get a living, breathing person to back you up, before opening that door. Unfortunately, I've never been accused of having too much in the common-sense department.

It occurred to me, just as I pushed the door open, that it wasn't locked. Emmy had stressed that this was off-limits to all but those in management, so it was to remain locked up tight whenever no one was in there.

'We've got payroll information in here, personnel files – lots of things that shouldn't be public knowledge. If you ever need to be in here, AJ, be sure to lock it behind you,' she had told me as we toured the Miramar. I had nodded solemnly, noting it as *muy importante.*

The memory gave me pause, wondering if Stan West was so lax that he'd not bothered to follow what I'd thought to be Miramar protocol.

The clicking sound was coming from one of the computers standing on a pair of desks. I moved around so that I could see the screen, but it was dark. The noise emanated from the computer tower, and as I bent closer to get a better idea of the source, the room went black. I felt myself falling across the desk, my legs buckling under me.

Someone had turned out my lights.

I can remember being knocked out one time before, the day that Ellie and I decided to try out for the Jackson

Elementary boys' baseball team. I'd managed to make contact with the ball, but as I ran to first base, Barney McKenzie, terror of the Fourth Grade, had beaned me on the back of the head with a perfectly aimed throw. That had effectively ended my plan to take over the team with my awesome baseball skills.

The light, when I started to stir, seemed watery, as if it was being filtered through the glass of an aquarium. When I managed to get my eyes opened all the way, I knew right away I wasn't in the office. The air smelled different, almost like over-brewed coffee. Another thing was wrong, too: I couldn't feel my hands, and my feet seemed to be welded together. A few more seconds and it was apparent that whoever had hit me also wanted to make sure that I wouldn't be able to go for help. My feet were tied tightly together and my hands had been trussed as well, so firmly that my fingers had lost all circulation. In short, I was in a world of hurt.

'So. You've decided to join us, I see,' said a voice that was oddly familiar.

I attempted to turn my head in the direction of whoever it was, but the room began to spin and I had to put my head back down. Once the ceiling had stopped in its orbit and I could focus again, I slid my eyes sideways, hoping to catch a glimpse of my captor.

From the corner of eye, I could see a pair of feet clad in soft-soled shoes. The ankles were slim, as were the legs. When they begin to move directly into my line of sight, I was so shocked that I couldn't think of a response.

Maria, shy employee of the Miramar and concerned friend, stood there, one eyebrow raised in contempt. Behind her stood Fernando, his large frame almost entirely blocking out the dim light coming in from a small window. How did ... I didn't understand ... my mind was not computing what my eyes were seeing. The Miramar Murderer was not just one person: it was a two-headed monster.

'Why, Maria? I mean, killing three people? And sending your thugs to beat up Ellie? What did you have to gain?' I tried to make sense of everything, trying to see Maria, kind, gentle Maria, as a killer. Fernando maybe, since the guy already seemed a bit off-kilter, but Maria? Ellie would never believe it.

Maria gave a short laugh that did not sound amused. 'Gain, AJ? What did I have to gain?' Her tone was mocking.

'Are you referring to the money I get from my little ID card business? The office is the perfect place to stash the blank cards, isn't it, Fernando? Not to mention telling us which engagements Emmy would be attending and who is on duty. *And* we can check which rooms are empty, so we can move the portable card reader and gear around. You'll have guessed,' she added, 'that locked doors are not a problem for me.'

Fernando had the grace to look uncomfortable. She continued in the same tone, 'Or is it freedom, the freedom to move around without fear of being caught by the police and sent back? If that's what you're talking about, then yes, I'm glad I did it.' She looked at me defiantly, her eyes glittering slits of anger in her face.

I was thinking frantically, trying to come up with something that would persuade Maria to let me go. What did she think I knew, anyway? All I wanted to do was to get back home to my boring little town in one piece, Ellie by my side. In movies, the victim – which would be me – usually promised not to reveal the crime or the perpetrators – that would be the twosome standing in front of me – to the authorities. Of course, I couldn't think of a single time it worked, but what the heck? At that moment, I had no other recourse. I swallowed, my throat feeling curiously dry.

'Maria, Fernando. I know you really don't know much

about me, but I can promise you that I am a woman of my word. And I give you my word that, if you let me go, I will never, ever tell a single soul what's happened here. And I'll leave today.

Promise.' My voice sounded pleading in my ears, and I hoped that Maria would believe me.

She gave that unpleasant laugh again, turning to jab Fernando in the ribs. 'See? Didn't I tell you that she'd say that? Maybe I should start telling fortunes like her so-very-bright cousin.'

Fernando smiled grimly but still remained silent. I aimed my next words at him. 'Fernando, if she was OK with killing her own brother, think what she might do to you.'

I didn't get any further.

Maria's slap across my face made my brains feel like they were sloshing around inside my already woozy head. It made me mad, though, madder than I'd been in a long time. Well, if you didn't count how mad I'd been at David, that is. I had been pretty ticked off at him.

I peered around Maria, locking my eyes on Fernando's expressionless face. 'I mean it! You can get out of this now.' She sent another blow my way, this one stinging my cheeks and wrenching my neck sideways. The woman was definitely strong, probably from lifting all those trays she'd carried to my room.

'C'mon, Fernando, untie me.' This time I was ready for Maria, rolling onto my side and catching her hand on my shoulder. I'd had enough of the cuffs to my head.

Fernando, to my amazement, stepped forward one tiny, tentative step. It was obvious now who was the leader in this relationship; size was definitely no factor here. Maria, sensing Fernando's movement, swung around, hand raised as if to hit him as well. He shrank back, but didn't take his eyes off of her.

I gave it one more try. 'Fernando. She's going to let

you take the fall for all of this, she's going …' I broke off to concentrate on avoiding another blow.

Fernando moved around Maria so that he was in my line of sight. The look on his face was one of confusion; maybe my words had hit a target.

'Maria,' he began, speaking softly. 'Does she speak the truth?' He had directed the words at her but kept looking at me.

Now Maria's anger was directed at him. Hands on hips, the small woman appeared to grow right before my eyes. She'd make an efficient mom one of these days, I thought with grudging admiration. She had the technique down already.

'Fernando, with all we have been through together, you and I, how can you even believe something this *gringa* says?' She spat the words out as though they had a foul taste, turning her head to shoot a venomous look at me. I stared back, my heart and hope sinking. There was no getting through to her.

I felt, rather than heard, the explosive movement. The door behind Fernando flew open, two uniformed officers on either side of a battering ram and a short figure behind them.

'Did someone call for room service?' Sal Bacon, cavalry and all, had come to the rescue.

The Epilogue, or How the Entire Ugly Episode Ended

In case you're wondering, Sal is not equipped with superpowers of the heat-seeking kind. The woman, I will have to admit, is canny beyond belief. She'd taken the liberty of outfitting my cellphone and Ellie's with a tracking device, thinking that it might come in handy if we were to get separated. Boy, did it ever.

Once it had occurred to her that my position seemed odd, that I hadn't moved for quite a while from an area of the resort where I shouldn't be, Sal had alerted the San Blanco Police Department. Her reputation there was legendary, so there was no fuss when she'd asked for backup. And although I hadn't seen her right away, Annie was standing right behind her aunt, ready to take on my kidnappers single-handedly if she needed to. Although with an aunt like she has, I don't know why she'd even think that.

Ellie was nearly in tears when we were finally reunited in the resort's main lobby.

Stan West, looking as inefficient as always, stood watching the scene with mouth hanging open. I wanted to go over and shut it for him.

The upshot of the entire sordid story was this: Maria's uncles, the infamous Martinez brothers, had made the mistake of talking too freely in front of her. She'd demanded a piece of the action, threatening to turn them in if they didn't. One had refused – that would be Israel, whose body was buried near the resort. The other uncle, Danny, realizing that this chick meant business, persuaded the other three to let her take Israel's place in the group and take his cut of the profits.

Her brother, the feckless Miguel, had tumbled to the scheme and told Emmy. The list we'd found in the Palo Verde suite was one that Miguel had written out for her. He'd given her the original and had kept the sheet of paper that lay beneath the one he'd torn off, knowing that the writing could still be read. Angry at his sister, he left his position at the Miramar, probably thinking that distance would equal safety.

Emmy, angry at the whole set-up, especially since it was being conducted at her beloved Miramar, confronted Maria. She'd shown her the list, effectively sealing her fate. A swift blow to the side of her head ended her life as well as the immediate threat of exposing Maria for the killer she was.

'Finding the letter', as Maria had claimed to do, was nothing but a phony put-up. She'd written it herself, hoping to steer all suspicion away from her. It had almost worked, too, until Danny was unsuccessful in getting rid of me and Ellie; he'd told Maria in no uncertain terms that he was not about to take the fall alone.

When Baird, Maria's PD stooge, wasn't able to finish the job, she'd gone into hyper-drive, convincing Stan West to call me to ask for my help. Little Maria, it would seem, had her fingers in every available pie. With that maneuver accomplished, it was just a matter of time.

I was just glad for everything to finally be over. I was more than ready to get the heck out of Dodge and head for them thar hills, as Daniel Boone might say. Besides, there's nothing wrong with my family that a little time can't fix.

Or maybe not. In any case, I was on my way back to where I belonged, where everyone knows everyone else and their kids, and where I felt loved. Yes, I even missed seeing my goofy family and all the equally nutty relatives.

I checked the calendar on my phone. If Ellie and I left tomorrow at the crack of dawn, I'd make it there for the last day of the Burnette Family Fiasco.

And after what I've just been through, talking and eating with a few nutcases sounds pretty nice. I'll take a roomful of Burnettes over any number of Marias and dimpled ex-detectives any ol' day. My family may not be perfect, but they're mine.

I just need to get a story together, though. They'll never believe what happened at the Miramar, chalking it up to my over-active imagination. I wonder if I can get Sal to … nah. It's better to end this right here and now. As my mother often says, 'Silence is a virtue.'

And I'm beginning to feel quite virtuous …

Also by Dane McCaslin

Becklaw's Murder Mystery Tour

For more information about **Dane McCaslin**
and other **Accent Press** titles
please visit

www.accentpress.co.uk

Lightning Source UK Ltd
Milton Keynes UK
UKOW06n1922271115

263659UK00001B/13/P